PLAYING BY THE RULES

Confessions of a Serial Dater

Scarlett Sixsmith

L J Warwick

Cover design by: LJ Warwick

ISBN 9798623299826

Independently Published

To Ash & Beth who roll their eyes at my antics a little too often. I'm so proud of you. I love you kids and your kids. At least I got something right x

To my ex's from whom I learned so much, mostly about myself. Thanks for all the fun and for all the lessons learned. Sometimes they were a little harsh but no hard feelings. My heart's stronger for the scar tissue.

To my Mr Right, will you please hurry up and make yourself known, I'm getting on a bit here!

CONTENTS

CHAPTER ONE

Finding yourself single in your forties after being in a long term relationship can be tough, but at least we now have the joys of technology assisted dating to help us find our potential Mr Right. There are many dating sites just bursting with weird and wonderful people dying to hook up with you. They're all there for their own reasons, some just want sex, some are married and are looking for a bit on the side, some are just after an ego boost but secretly I'm a bit of a romantic at heart and so I'd like to think that the majority of people are genuine and looking for love. We all just want to love and be loved, right?

So I'd joined the dating sites, quite a few of them and became a prolific dater. Not by choice mind you, I just couldn't find anyone I had that spark with, that all important chemistry. I also managed to arrange dates with quite a few not-rights who were just pretending to be normal. I suppose it didn't help matters that I wasn't really sure what it was I was looking for but I knew with certainty what it was I didn't want and that was to end up back in a miserable relationship with someone who never made any effort. A relationship is a two way street and I was fed up of being the one that made all the effort. I believe in love. I believe in trust and respect and honesty and loyalty. I believe in caring and looking after one another, communication and being there for each other. Oh and a good sex life is high on my wish list too. A tall order for Tinder maybe so I just concentrated on having a bit of fun at first with the hope that one day I might find the rest. Ultimately I was hoping to find my Mr Right, but I was happy to enjoy time with various Mr Right Nows until he turned up. If he ever did.

After almost a year of dating fails, disappointments and heartbreaks, some good sex, some great sex and some very, very bad sex I finally found a man that I liked, connected with and who was fantastic in bed. And, bonus prize, he was very well hung. Hurrah! I was having the best sex of my life with someone whom I probably never would have considered a relationship with or even met in the first place if it hadn't been for internet dating. I did things I never would have even contemplated before, good and bad and sometimes against my better judgement. He took me on a scenic journey of sexual exploration, it was a journey that was exciting, frustrating and scary and which took me out of my comfort zone many times. I became totally addicted to this man but like all addictions, it wasn't healthy and it didn't end well.

This is that story.

CHAPTER TWO

My amazing lover was Ben. I'd connected with him on OKCupid. To be perfectly honest I hadn't really been interested in him at first. I studied his profile pictures and decided he just wasn't for me, not the type of man that I found attractive. I know looks aren't everything and I hate to sound shallow but I'm sure you agree with me that there does have to be some attraction there. I almost deleted his message without a reply but I had been a little bored, his message was nice and so I had messaged him back. I didn't at that point have any desire or intention to actually meet up with him but I did like to chat with people sometimes, it helped while away the hours when there was nothing else to keep you entertained.

We exchanged a few initial messages via the dating app. He asked me about my situation and I explained how I had been mostly single for the last year or so after my ten year relationship had broken down when I had discovered that my partner had been cheating on me. He said he was sorry to hear that I had gone through such heart-break and told me he was still facing his. I was unsure what he meant by this and so I asked him if he could explain further. He asked if it was OK for us to chat on the telephone, he told me his situation was an unusual one and he would like to explain it to me properly so there would be no ambiguity or confusion. I didn't usually swap numbers until I got to know someone a bit better via messaging but something about him (and the fact that I am more than a little bit nosy) made me want to learn more. So I agreed, gave him my number and he called me almost straight away.

"Good evening beautiful, how are you?" he said when I answered " Look at us both stuck in on a Saturday night on our own. Sad isn't it? Thank you for replying to my message, I honestly didn't think you would as you're completely out of my league."

He sounded nice and I was flattered by his compliments. "Thank you," I replied, " but I don't think I'm out of your league at all!"

"Well it's not often a woman as beautiful as you replies to me, in fact it's a first." he said.

Was I really that beautiful? It was nice that he said so and although I don't consider myself to be ugly and I do try to make an effort I just think I'm average looking really, nothing special. As I said, I was flattered but I was wary. I'd become wise to some of the tactics some guys used to reel you in.

Maybe he was just a smooth talker and said things like that to all the women he spoke to.

We chatted some more about the usual, inconsequential things you talk about with a stranger. What we did for a living, (he was a construction manager), what music, films and food we liked. We appeared to have quite a lot in common and conversation flowed easily between us. He came across as very intelligent, actually showed an interest in what I had to say and was quite entertaining. He began to tell me about the fact that he used to be a prolific participant on the swinging scene, sharing some sometimes shocking, sometimes amusing stories about his sexual exploits over the years. He certainly was sexually very experienced. Now here's a man who should be good in bed I thought to myself.

"At the risk of blowing my own trumpet I'm very good in bed and I'm also blessed to be very well endowed" he said with a chuckle as if he was reading my mind. This gets even better I thought. It was a shame I didn't really find him attractive.

He started to explain to me about his unusual situation at home. It went something like this:

He had met a woman, Gina, about eight or so years previously on the swinging scene. They'd had an open, fairly casual relationship continuing to see other people but got on really well with each other and so decided to move in together. He bought a house and she moved in with him but almost straight away he said he knew he had made a mistake. There was just no real passion there, he explained, no real connection, they found they weren't really all that compatible and although they continued with the relationship for a while, both of them finding their passion elsewhere, shared and solo, cracks began to appear. They started to argue and fall out. After a couple of years Ben came to the decision that he wanted out of the relationship and he accepted a two year contract to go and work in London. He told Gina she could stay in the house whilst he was in London but that she would have to find her own place before he moved back.

So off he went to work down in London and he absolutely hated it. Not used to big city living he was miserable and lonely there. In the meantime Gina tragically became very poorly with a terminal illness that was affecting her heart, causing it to slowly fail. When he found out how sick she was Ben cut short his contract in London and returned to Manchester finding work nearer to home so he could be there to help to look after her.

"Our relationship is purely platonic" he explained to me, "We don't even share the same bedroom. Although I don't want to be in a romantic relationship with her, we are still close and I care about her very much as a friend. She has nowhere else to go, hasn't got very long to live and so I let her stay in my house. She's basically my lodger. I like to be upfront about the situation from the start because obviously I'm living with someone and it would look bad if someone I was seeing discovered that and I hadn't fully explained it."

I pondered his story. It was a very unusual situation but he did sound believable. If he was married or had a significant other why would he make up such a complicated story? He could just do what other unfaithful guys tend to do the world over and pretend that she didn't exist.

"So what does Gina think of you having relationships with other women?" I asked.

"She is absolutely fine with it," he replied "in fact she encourages it. We are just close friends now who care for each other and she wants me to be happy. Obviously though it's not a great time for me to get into something overly serious so I'm really just looking for something casual. It would be unfair for me to commit to someone right now when I already have a commitment to Gina, I promised I would see it through to the end with her so she won't be alone. She's been given less than a year to live, frankly she's that poorly right now I'll be surprised if she sees Christmas."

"That's very sad, you must be a very special kind of person to give her that kind of commitment and support."

"I don't consider myself to be special. It's just what any decent person would do I would hope."

I would hope so too but people all too often made a sharp exit when faced with difficult situations. "So, what is it you are looking for relationship wise?" I asked, changing the subject "How casual is casual?"

"Well I hate hookups and one night stands." He said, which was how I felt about them too "I'm looking for something that's a little more meaningful but with someone who understands that I can't offer any commitment right now. Sex is so much better when you have a connection with someone don't you think? It would just be casual though, at least for the time being, but hopefully caring and honest. I do have an open relationship with another woman named Ellen who I've been seeing occasionally for the past two years or so and of course I wouldn't expect anyone I was seeing to be monogamous. It would be fine by me for them to date others."

This sounded possibly what I was looking for too right then. More of a friends with benefits arrangement than anything serious. I wasn't looking to jump into a serious relationship after just getting out of a miserable long term one. I wanted more than just a hookup though, and I agreed, sex was much better with someone you had a connection with. It would be nice to have regular good sex with someone but still be able to continue to date and look for something more without having to hide it. I'd had friends with benefits arrangements before and they had worked fine for a while, had been mutually satisfying. There had never been any danger that I would ever fall in love with either of the guys and both relationships had eventually ended for very different reasons but with no heartbreak, at least not on my part.

We chatted a little while longer and then I surprised myself by agreeing to meet him for a date. Even though I'd originally had no intention of meeting up with him it seemed we were looking for the same things and after talking to him on the phone for a few hours I was intrigued by him and I wanted to learn more about him.

We met at a hotel a couple of days later. When I first saw him I must admit I didn't find him physically attractive at all. Quite short, smallish build, someone who had once obviously been bigger but age and laziness about his physical health had left him looking somehow worn and diminished. He looked older than his 45 years. It wasn't that he was ugly, just really nothing special. Another tired looking, middle aged man who faded into the background. I couldn't believe this was the same man I had been talking with on the phone for hours the other night. This was the prolific swinger? The sexually experienced, very well endowed guy? I could definitely vouch for the fact he was blessed in that department at least, as he had sent me (after politely asking if it was OK to do so first) a short video showcasing his impressive assets. In fact, I'm embarrassed to say, that was one of the deciding factors in me agreeing to meet him. I'd never dated a man with such a large penis and I wondered what it would feel like to have sex with him. In retrospect, he probably used that often to try to entice women to meet him as he was certainly nothing special in the looks department. Well it worked on this greedy, horny woman anyway.

When I first laid eyes on him I'm ashamed to say I briefly considered leaving without acknowledging him but he noticed me before I could do so. He looked over at me and I decided that as I was there I may as well stay and have a drink with him. He smiled at me as I approached him. He did have a nice smile, his eyes crinkling invitingly, his teeth were slightly crooked but that strangely added to his appeal. Close up I could see his short brown hair was going a little wispy on top but he was not yet going bald and his eyes were a bit of a muddy colour, somewhere between green and brown. He was clean shaven, dressed nicely, smart but casual in jeans and shirt, smelled amazing, was very considerate and had very good manners. He appeared to be a rare, real gentleman. I'd expected our date to last an hour or so at the very most and then to part ways with the "Nice to meet you but you're not really for me" line and never see him again but we were there for several hours talking non stop. I didn't want it to come to an end. I was totally confused by my feelings. The chemistry between us was amazing, I was almost overwhelmed with desire for this ordinary looking man. We had barely touched, only once when he'd asked permission to touch my skin to see if it felt as soft as it looked. His touch had electrified me. We exchanged a very chaste kiss goodbye but he had left me tingling with desire and a longing to see him again.

We quickly arranged a second date, just two days later. We met up and he took me to a swingers club. Swinging was something I'd always been curious about and I'd expressed an interest in seeing a club so he'd offered to take me. It was a strange venue for a second date I suppose, certainly something you would never forget. It was a very surprising experience, nothing like I was expecting. I went in half scared to death and feeling totally self-conscious but came out feeling sexually liberated and firmly on my journey down the road to my addiction with Ben.

The club had been nothing like I thought it would be. We didn't have sex with any other people, I'd insisted that that wasn't on the cards, not that night anyhow. He just took my hand, showed me around and then after a steamy necking session in the bubbling hot tub we had amazing, kinky sex in a private room. It had been mind blowing. With his experience and the sexual chemistry we had between us I had been hoping it would be good but let me tell you, it totally exceeded all my expectations. He made me orgasm multiple times and as I lay there afterwards spent and sweating I wondered what on earth had just happened. I looked at him, my brain failing to make the connection between this man and the exquisite feelings my body had just experienced. I realised he was probably going to be the best lover I'd ever had. Second date and I was already hooked.

CHAPTER THREE

I was very much looking forward to seeing Ben again after our date at the swinger's club. Although we had agreed that our relationship would be an open one where we could both continue to see other people my head was just too full of him and the amazing sex we'd had. Checking the dating sites hadn't even crossed my mind since I'd met him, I was more than happy to explore the potential with just Ben, the first taste had been tantalising and I was excited to see what the rest of the journey would bring with it.

It was a sunny, autumnal Thursday, the day after the swinger's club date and I couldn't help to keep thinking about the night before. Everytime I thought about it, which was I estimated about every three and a half minutes on average, I got that delicious clench down below and hyperactive butterflies in my stomach. I couldn't concentrate on anything, least of all work.

My phone rang, Ben. Grinning like a fool I answered. "Good morning."

"Good morning beautiful, how are you?" He asked.

"Great, I can't stop thinking about last night" I replied, there was that clench again. I didn't think I'd been that horny since I was a teenager.

"And?"

"And, I'm not getting much work done today! I'm looking forward to a repeat session."

He laughed "Me too, very much so. How about Sunday? Back at the hotel? Eightish?"

"Perfect."

"Great, I'll book a room."

"I'll look forward to it."

The rest of the week dragged, Sunday seemed to take forever to come around, I just couldn't wait to see him. He rang and video called me several times. We never seemed to run out of things to talk about and we chatted for hours. I had allocated a ringtone to his contact details - Playtime it seemed appropriate. Just hearing the first couple of notes of Playtime set off the fanny flutters because I knew it was Ben calling.

Finally, at long last it was Sunday night. After a long shower, making sure all the right bits were stubble free and squeaky clean I packed a small overnight bag, got dressed in some kinky new underwear and a long red dress that showed off my figure, especially my best assets, my breasts. Then I carefully applied my makeup and made a brave attempt to make my hair behave. After blow drying and back combing and spraying and resigning myself to the fact that that was as good as it got I applied a vampy new red lipstick that matched my dress and stood back to appraise my reflection in the bathroom mirror. “You’ll do” I told myself and winked at Walter, my old ginger tomcat who was sitting on the side of the bath watching me. Walter just yawned and stretched in response then jumped down onto the floor mat and started licking his arse. Charming.

It was a lovely, late summer evening, still warm with a blue sky that had small fluffy white clouds scattered about. I took several deep breaths smiling to myself barely containing my excitement and bemused by my eagerness to see Ben. It had been a very long time since someone had had such an effect on me and my lady bits. Stomach churning, fanny fluttering I got into my car and set off to the hotel, I was going to be very early, which was unusual for me, but I simply could not wait in the house any longer. I arrived at the hotel at seven thirty thinking I would have a drink in the bar to settle my nerves a little whilst I waited for Ben to arrive, but when I walked into the lobby he was already sitting there looking at his phone. He must have been eager too. He looked up and saw me “Hello sexy” he said standing to kiss me, then, standing back, his hands resting lightly on my shoulders he took a long look at me “You look gorgeous.” he told me.

I flushed with pleasure both at the compliment

and of seeing him "Thank you" I said.

Taking hold of my overnight bag in one hand and holding my hand with his free one he led me into the hotel bar. "What would you like to drink?" He asked as I settled into a large comfortable leather chair in a fairly secluded corner. I wondered if it would be inappropriate to ask if we could just go straight up to the room, decided that it might be so I asked for a glass of Rosè.

I looked around the bar at the other people whilst I waited for Ben to come back with our drinks. It was quite noisy and fairly busy. There were a lot of couples there. I wondered how many of them were having affairs or were on dates. You could tell the ones who had probably been together a long time as they were mostly ignoring each other, distracted by mobile phones. A pretty woman in her thirties sitting fairly close by was talking away animatedly to a plain, overweight man sitting with her. Her husband maybe. He was ignoring her choosing instead to give his attention to his phone, engrossed by the little screen. She chatted regardless, either resigned to his rudeness or too polite to say anything to him about it. I wondered why she put up with it. Ben came back fairly quickly "Cheers!" he said as he handed me my drink before sitting down and raising his glass towards me "Here's to good sex."

"I'll drink to that." I said smiling and raising my glass towards him "Cheers!"

We sat in the bar just chatting about our week

and sipping our drinks. We discussed a film we had both recently seen agreeing it was very good but I was finding it hard to concentrate fully on the conversation because I was very horny. After about half an hour or so Ben gently placed his hand on my leg under the table, pushing my skirt up a little and rubbing my thigh through the thin nylon material of my hold-ups. His touch electrified me, making me tingle all over. I looked at him and smiled, feeling my cheeks flush a little as we made eye contact and he smiled back at me.

"Stockings?" He enquired. I nodded, yes. His smile turned into a grin. "I think it's time to go upstairs." he said.

I agreed. I finished my drink in one big gulp and almost sent myself dizzy standing up too fast in my eagerness. "Let's go." I said.

He stood, picked up my bag, took hold of my hand and we walked over to the lift that took us to the second floor. He had already checked in, room 223 was all ours for the night. Using a key card he opened the door and let me into the room. It was quite small but it was nice, well appointed and dominated by a huge bed that looked to be very comfortable. There was a bottle of wine chilling in a cooler with a single wine glass next to it on one of the bedside tables and a bottle of water with a glass tumbler on the other side. Ben didn't drink alcohol, didn't like being drunk and losing control he'd told me. I on the other hand enjoyed the uninhibited feeling I got after a few drinks. I was by nature a sometimes anxious person, a bit of a worrier so I liked to be able to let go, relax and enjoy myself occasionally with the help of a drink. With alcohol, admittedly, my stop button sometimes didn't work and things occasionally got a little out of hand. I often ended up making a complete arse of myself. I made a mental note not to drink too much that night.

I stood by the side of the bed whilst Ben dimmed the lights a little and found a radio channel on the TV so we could have a little background music. He poured me a glass of wine, handed it to me and I took a couple of sips before placing it on the dressing table. He walked slowly towards me then pulled me close to him and we kissed for a while after which he pulled my dress off over my head. I was wearing red lace underwear and black hold up stockings underneath which delighted Ben. He stood back and admired me in my underwear from all angles for some time, licking then biting his bottom lip, his eyes roaming all over my body. "Mmm very, very nice." he murmured "I think we'll leave those on for now"

He pulled his belt free from the loops in his jeans and placed it on the bed. "I think we may need that later." he said looking at me with a little smile. We'd had a conversation the night before about BDSM, although personally I'd never gone further than a bit of mild spanking and being tied up on the odd occasion it was something that intrigued and excited me. Nothing too extreme mind you, I didn't want to get tied up with complicated knots that cut off my blood supply and then beaten senseless with a horse whip thank you but the idea of a forceful man and a little bit of rough play really got me going. I looked at the black leather belt lying on the bed in stark contrast to the crisp white linen and felt a little jolt of excitement.

Feeling a little self-conscious in just my underwear and heels, but horny as hell, Ben ordered me to unbutton his shirt. My hands were shaking a little as I did as I was told undoing the small white buttons and revealing his hairy chest. I know opinions are divided on man hair but I do like it. Hirsute men are definitely my cup of tea. I love to lie next to a man running my fingers through his furry chest hair and I like beards too, although the fact that they are said to contain more bacteria than the average dogs arse does sometimes make me a little squeamish. Ben was very hairy, all over lovely soft curly body hair almost like a teddy bear but his face was always clean shaven. He freed his arms from his shirt and put it on a chair at the side of the bed then sat on the bed to take off his jeans and socks, leaving just his black boxers. I could see his erection straining to get free through the fabric. Standing up again he pulled me towards him and kissed me. We shared some more long, lingering kisses (he really was a great kisser) then he stood back, his hands on my upper arms and indicated the floor. "You said you like to be submissive," he said "show me. Kneel down and look up at me."

Kneel down? On the floor? Jesus, Hang on I'm getting on a bit here, I'm not exactly fit, my knees are not what they used to be and I've a dodgy hip, this was going to be hard work. What if I can't get back up again? All these thoughts were running through my mind but I got on my knees as I was told, although not very gracefully. I looked up at him, he held my gaze for a moment making me shiver his hands resting lightly on my shoulders. I wondered what he was thinking. "Good girl. Now get up" he ordered.

This was worse than going to a yoga class I thought as I used the bed to pull myself up and clamber back onto my feet. Next, picking up his belt, he told me to get on my knees once more but this time on the bed with my arse stuck up in the air. I did as I was told, holding my breath in anticipation as he walked behind me bouncing the belt off the palm of his hand. "I think you deserve six today." he told me.

I jumped as the leather struck my bum cheeks. It stung a little but it didn't really hurt. "One" said Ben. The belt hit me again "Two"

He continued all the way up to six by which time I was horny as hell. He placed the belt on the floor and ordered me to take off my underwear which I did without argument after which he told me to lie face down back on the bed. He straddled me and gently massaged my bum cheeks. "OK?" he asked "Did that hurt?"

"Only a little. But it felt good" I admitted.

He bent and kissed my stinging bum cheeks then my legs, then slowly kissed me all the way up my back. He got to the top of my back then spent a long time caressing and gently biting my neck and nibbling my earlobes. My ears are a major turn on for me. I just love having them nibbled, rubbed and licked. Although I wouldn't go as far as actual ear sex, I wouldn't fancy someone trying to stick their knob in there. Apparently that really is a thing but surely it must be a physical impossibility unless you have a seriously small dick? No thanks. No masterbating anywhere near my ear canal either thank you. Don't want an earful of spunk, could you imagine the nightmare trying to clean that out would be?

Ben lay on me so I was pinned against the bed unable to move under the weight of him. I could feel his dick, hard and ready for action against the top my thigh, teasing me. I was tingling all over with desire and almost climaxing just by him nibbling my ears and neck.

"Do you want this?" Ben whispered in my ear pushing his cock harder against my leg.

"Oh yes!" I whispered back. I did, I really did.

"What do you say?" He asked.

"Please. Yes please!"

He moved up a little, still pinning me face

down on the bed and slid inside me. “Sexy bitch” he growled in my ear, grabbing my hair in his fist and pulling it just a little harder than gently.

It didn’t take me long to climax, and again, and again before Ben climaxed too. He climbed off me and we lay close together, he on his back with me snuggled up to the side of him with my head on his chest saying nothing just enjoying the closeness of our sweaty naked bodies, exhilarated and shag happy. After a few minutes he kissed the top of my head and said “Babe, we need to talk”

Uh oh I thought, this is where he tells me he’s married or something.

“You know this is just a sex thing right?” he said.

“Yes.” I replied.

“Good.” he said, “We can’t be developing feelings for each other, things are just too complicated for me at the moment.”

“Of course, I know”

“Don’t be falling in love with me” he warned with a little laugh.

“Don’t worry” I said “I understand your situation. Besides, I’ve no intentions of falling in love with anyone right now.” Especially you, I thought to myself.

He smiled at me, stretched and got up off the bed. “Good, I’d hate anything to spoil what we have. I’ve got a great feeling about us, we are going to be so good together. I’m going to grab a shower, fancy joining me?”

I did fancy joining him. The bathroom boasted a large walk in shower that we both fitted in easily and we spent some pleasant time soaping each other under the warm spray. Afterwards I dried my hair wearing the hotel's bathrobe whilst Ben dried himself and got dressed. I felt a little disappointed, I was hoping we would be spending the night together and the disappointment must have shown on my face.

"Sorry babe" he said looking at me "I would love to spend the night here with you but I have to go. I can't leave Gina alone all night. She's too poorly."

Just a sex thing, I reminded myself swallowing my disappointment "Of course." I said "Thanks for a great evening."

"No, thank you. It was amazing, I can't wait for next time." He said, bending down to kiss me, "Sleep well, gorgeous creature, I'll call you in the morning."

He left and I clambered into the big bed alone. At least I had the wine to keep me company. I topped up my glass and lay there contemplating my relationship with Ben. I couldn't let my feelings get the better of me, I just had to enjoy it for what it was, just great sex, but I couldn't help wondering just what the hell I was letting myself in for.

CHAPTER FOUR

It was one of my favourite days of the month, Wine and Whine Wednesday. On the second Wednesday of the month the girls gather, have a few glasses of cheap plonk, fill each other in on the gossip and have a right good moan about whatever was pissing us off. A man or two usually featured there somewhere. We have been meeting up like this for about three years now. There are about eight of us in total but it is very rare we all get together every month as usually someone is ill / away/ no babysitter. Ladies were introduced to the group from time to time and others dropped out so the number was ever changing but there is a core group of four of us who have been friends for over twenty years now.

The four of us that make up the core of our ladies group are a bit of a diverse lot - Jill is in her late thirties, an absolutely drop dead gorgeous blonde with a stunning curvy figure and an eternally sunny outlook on life. Usually looks like hers would provoke jealousy in some people but everybody loves her, you can't help yourself, she's just so nice, and funny too. She is a primary school teacher and looks like butter wouldn't melt but she has the most outrageous sex with a seemingly never ending string of beautiful girl-friends.

Julie, mid forties, divorced mother of two of the most horrible children you could ever have the misfortune of meeting. Tall, slim, short red hair, very intelligent, amazing career at one of the major banks. Always a bundle of nerves but a lovely, loyal friend. I'd stayed with her briefly after my relationship with my long term partner Danny had broken down and I'd nowhere to go. She'd readily welcomed me into her home and said I could stay as long as I needed to for which I'd be eternally grateful but I'd been motivated to find a place of my own pretty sharpish and had almost required a prozac prescription after spending time living with her two boys.

Becky was in her late forties, another teacher. Short, plump, and matronly. Dark chestnut hair cut in a shiny bob. The most patient person I'd ever known. Amazing cook. Been happily married for over twenty years to Paul with teenage identical twin girls who are as lovely as she is, her mini-me's.

Then there's me - mid forties, divorced since forever, tragic love life, arty, scatty, writer / illustrator. One amazing grown up daughter who became the parent in our single parent household from age nine because I was a bit useless at being an adult. Short arse, long dark hair, curvy, with a face often described as 'cute' or 'adorable'. Seriously! I don't want to be adorable or cute, I want to be beautiful and sexy. But you've got to work with what you're given I suppose.

Sometimes we met at the pub. Sometimes, if it was a special occasion we would meet at our favourite Italian or Indian restaurant and sometimes we went to someone's home. This Wednesday we had all been invited round to Shona's. Great.

Don't get me wrong, I love Shona, it's just that, well, she's a bit odd. More than a bit odd. She joined our group about six years ago when she met Jill at an anti-fracking demonstration. She's been happily married to Jed since forever, they've got loads of kids about seven or eight I think but I've lost count. She's been pregnant so many times that people have started saying "again?" instead of "congratulations!" when she announces she's up the duff. She always seems to have a baby or toddler dangling off a boob and a slightly larger child with a snotty nose wrapped around her leg. Considering she's so concerned about the environment she doesn't seem to think there's anything wrong with adding to the already overpopulated world. Despite having a house full of hyperactive small people she has time to make everything herself. Badly. Food, clothes, wine and even terrible arts and crafts which she proudly displays all over the house. Sadly she's not much better at cooking than she is at art, even her best effort, her bread, is tasteless and curiously hard and chewy "Shona's rustic bread is like eating an old flip-flop" is how Jill describes it.

She is totally unencumbered by any style or fashion sense and wears a collection of homemade elasticated waist skirts that accommodate her forever pregnant tummy in a selection of loud floral patterns coupled with men's t-shirts that drown her petite frame. You rarely see anything but flat brown sandals on her feet no matter what the weather is doing. She never wears any makeup and I've not seen her frizzy blonde hair in any style other than scraped up into a messy bun. Her wine tastes like cat's piss and I suspect more than one glassful has been sneakily poured into the pot of one of the many plants that are dotted around the house. I was guilty of doing this on more than one occasion. I have long given up on murdering plants at home, even when I lavish care on them and look after them properly they just curl up and die on me but Shona's plants appear to thrive on the bad wine.

Shona's hubby Jed is something big and successful in music production. He knows lots of famous people and quite often Shona will just casually throw into conversation the fact that a certain famous rock or pop star had popped over to the house. I would be totally starstruck if I found myself in the company of some of these people but I guess it is just something she is used to. Jed and Shona live in a gorgeous big house that has been converted from a pub with their ever increasing offspring and a ménagerie of bizarre animals including stinky little white mice, rabbits, cats, hedgehogs, an old dog named Buzz and a herd of alpacas. The alpacas are all named after prime ministers, at the last count they had Maggie, Gordon, Winston, Tony and Clement all living in a field at the back of the house.

Odd though she is, I have to say Shona is lovely, always happy and optimistic, nothing ever seems to get her down. Her and Jed are totally, puke-inducingly in love with each other and she is totally content with her lot. She is loving and kind and always has time for a brew and a chat if you need an ear to listen or a shoulder to cry on.

Jill and I shared a taxi over to Shona's, each cradling a bottle of wine, Californian Zinfandel for me and French Chardonnay for Jill. "I hope Shona hasn't had time to make the dandelion wine she's been threatening us with" said Jill. Dandelion wine, was that even a thing? It seemed Shona could make bad wine out of just about anything but none of us had the heart to tell her just how awful it was.

"I hope she's not had time to bake any scones" I said and we both started to laugh. Last time I'd had one of Shona's scones I'd broken a tooth on it and ended up cutting an ex's penis on the sharp edge whilst giving him a blow job. He bled a bit but it wasn't a mortal wound, I'm sure his dick is still in fine working order. He hadn't been impressed but to be fair he'd deserved it, the guy is a cockwomble of the highest order.

We arrived at Shona's to find Becky already there. She had a glass of wine in hand and judging by the way she was gingerly sipping at it I guessed it was the dreaded dandelion variety. She was sitting near a large healthy rubber plant and her glass was almost empty, I smiled knowingly at her and she smiled back with a slight nod.

"Scarlett, Jill!" exclaimed Shona enthusiastically, kissing and hugging us both, (she is a very tactile person) and relieving us of our bottles. "Let's put that in the fridge, and I'll grab you both a glass of chilled stuff. I didn't have time to make the dandelion wine but luckily we had a couple of bottles of nettle left over" Oh joy, nettle wine. Yummy. Off she floated to the kitchen returning a couple of minutes later with two large glasses. I sipped it. Yep, cat piss. I sat within arm's length of a large healthy Yucca.

About ten minutes later Tanya arrived. Tanya is a very successful, high powered business woman who frankly, I find more than a little scary and intimidating. She doesn't seem to have much in common with the rest of us but appears to like hanging around with us non the less. Nobody can quite remember how she became a part of our group, she just seemed to show up one day and no one will take responsibility for befriending her. She assumes the role of Boss Lady of the group and admittedly is great at getting us all organised when we go on trips or venture further afield than normal on a night out. She is married to Mark who we all secretly referred to as "Poor Mr Tanya " and has two perfect teenaged boys who she hardly ever sees because she shipped them off to boarding school as soon as they were old enough. Shona didn't hug Tanya, she knew better than to try, I don't think Tanya ever hugged or had any physical contact with anyone, not even Poor Mr Tanya. We used to joke that she used a turkey baster in between meetings to get pregnant with her two boys, or that she simply purchased them off the dark web, genetically engineered perfect babies.

"Would you like a glass of wine?" Shona asked Tanya

"Did you make it?"

"Yes."

"God, no. No offence but your wine tastes like crap." said Tanya bluntly, pulling two bottles of Prosecco from a carrier bag "I'll have some of this."

I didn't know whether to be shocked at Tanya's blunt honesty or admire it but Shona wasn't fazed at all by her rudeness. She just took the bottles from Tanya and went to the kitchen to pour her a glass.

Once we were all settled with our drinks and all the kids were in bed apart from the smallest who was snoozing between breastfeeds in a well used carrycot on the kitchen table we started to catch up with each other. I was bringing the girls up to date on my latest dating adventures and was telling them about Ben.

"You really like him don't you?" said Shona

"She really likes his enormous cock!" laughed Jill

"Sounds amazing. Glad you're getting some decent sex at last." said Becky "D'ya know, I've not had sex since I was preggers with the twins."

We all looked at her in shock at this revelation. Her girls were fifteen.

"You've not had a shag in over fifteen years?" questioned Jill. "Seriously? Bloody hell. Why not? Was the birth that traumatic?"

Becky shrugged, "The birth was fine, well, as fine as it could be considering I was squeezing the equivalent of two bowling balls out of my poor vagina one after another. The stitches weren't much fun either but they healed well. I just don't really like it. Sex I mean. Never have done. I love Paul to pieces but sex wise we're just not compatible." she explained

"In what way?" asked Tanya.

"Well he likes sex, a lot, I don't. He's a bit kinky in the bedroom but it's not for me. Simple as that really." explained Becky. "We sat and had a good talk after the girls were born and I agreed that he could go elsewhere for his oats as long as he was discreet about it. So he has his girlfriends, I know about them and I'm fine with it, I've even met a couple of them in the past, they were nice. Apart from one woman that is who he met in church. She acted all virtuous but in reality she was just a dick eating monster. I soon made sure he got rid of that one."

"But what if he fell in love with one of his girlfriends and left you for her?" asked Shona

"If he does, he does." said Becky matter of factly "There's no guarantees with any relationship are there? I love him and I know he loves me. We kiss and cuddle are very affectionate with each other and are very close but I just don't want to have sex with him. Or anybody else for that matter. If I didn't let him have sex elsewhere then he'd leave me anyway. I understand he has his needs and I'm happy for someone else to see to those. I just don't want to know any of the finer details."

"Don't you feel jealous?" I asked, I know I probably would have if I had a husband and he had been sleeping with other women.

"No, not really. He's honest with me about who he's with when he's not at home and he spends lots of quality time with me and the girls. We're very happy. He's a loving husband and an amazing father. I think we have reached the perfect compromise."

I was wondering if it would be acceptable to ask in what way he was kinky when Jill beat me to the question. "You said he's a bit Kinky? Paul? I mean it's not really any of our business but really?! How, in what way? I just can't imagine it!"

"He likes to be pissed on. And he likes to be dominated. Frankly the thought of whipping his spotty, saggy old arse is more than I can bear." said Becky "As for pissing on him, I tried it once when we were first married but I just worried about the mess. It took me half an hour to squeeze out a little tiny drop and it almost made me physically sick. I'm more than happy for someone else to take care of that side of things with him for me."

My mind pictured quiet, bespectacled, tubby, accountant Paul in one of his rumpled suits. Wow, who would have thought it? It's always the quiet ones!

CHAPTER FIVE

October was drawing to an end and although the weather was still quite pleasant there was a real chill in the air early in the morning and in the evenings when the sun disappeared. It was the morning after our regular ladies get-together and I was feeling a little worse for wear after having one too many glasses of wine as per usual. I had a looming deadline so I'd gotten up early, well - early for me, with the intention of getting a good day's work done. I even got dressed and fired up the laptop instead of lolling around in my pyjamas half the day faffing about with my iPad. I was editing the most boring academic text book ever about some sort of ancient civilisation that had been written by someone who hadn't yet discovered spell check and didn't understand punctuation and I was finding it difficult not to fall asleep at my desk. My phone bleeped, ooh distraction!

Text message off Jill -

Off today, do you fancy pub lunch?

Sorry can't do today too much work on. Pub 2morrow?

Aww, no worries, tomorrow is good. Don't work too hard x

I was very tempted, I really did fancy lunch in the pub but with Jill and a couple of cheap gins it would inevitably stretch into a good three hours and I just couldn't afford the time if I wanted to meet my deadline and get paid so I could pay my rent on time and buy essentials like wine.

I got stuck back into my work but ten minutes later there was a knock at the door. Bloody hell, who was this now? I was annoyed at the interruption. No one ever comes round during the day. I saved the document I was working on and went to the door, opening it to be confronted with the most enormous, over the top bouquet of flowers I'd ever seen in my life held by a grinning delivery man/boy of indeterminate age wearing a baseball cap, t-shirt and shorts and sporting an impressive bushy beard. I'd never seen so many flowers in one bouquet, it was like all the flowers I'd never been given before had all suddenly turned up at once.

"Flowers!" announced the man/boy just in case I hadn't noticed, shoving the impressive blooms in my face.

"For me?" I asked

"Scarlett, number 17, if that's you then yep they're yours."

I was amazed, no one ever sent me flowers. Taking them from the delivery man/boy I hefted them inside, put them on the coffee table and looked for a card. Nestled in between the blooms was a small card with a picture of a love heart with two words written on it: ***sexy bitch.*** I grinned, Ben. I had given him my address on Saturday so he could come and pick me up this Sunday to go to the club again. Picking up my phone I sent him a message -

Thank you so much
they're beautiful xx

My phone pinged back straight away

What are? X

The flowers, totally over
the top must have cost
you a fortune but they're
gorgeous xx

Not that you don't deserve
them but not from me babe X

What? If not from Ben then who on earth would send me such expensive flowers? And who else would call me a sexy bitch?

Puzzled, I made a coffee, my fourth mug of the morning and sat back at my desk. I tried to get back to work but kept looking at the flowers distracted, trying to think who they could be from.

I formed a mental list and went down it crossing names off.

Chris an ex friend with benefits? He'd been a bit upset when I called it a day and I still got the occasional message from him asking if he could see me but he never had any money and the only buds he ever bought were the ones he could smoke.

Pete, my other ex friend with benefits? Professional fuckwit with no shame. Definitely not from him. He always called me darlin' and his idea of romance was to send you a close up dick pic with a message asking you if you fancied a fuck at one am.

Liam the undertaker who I'd had a brief relationship with earlier in the year? He was a nice guy but the master of ridiculous dirty talk, liked to be called 'daddy' not great in bed and totally OCD. He had tried really hard and long to get back with me so he could be a possibility but I hadn't heard from him in a long while, the over the top flowers just didn't seem his style and he had always called me baby, never sexy bitch.

Rob, another ex that had moved away with work? Again not really his style. We were still in touch occasionally, we still cared about each other and had a lot of history together going back over twenty years but our relationship was firmly in the friends zone now.

Connor? Lovely, sexy, gorgeous, Connor from America. My summer fantasy romance. I allowed myself a moment or two reminiscing about the fantastic few weeks I had spent with him earlier in the summer, smiling wistfully to myself. We'd had an amazing time together and not just in bed. He had been great company but it had definitely been just a holiday romance and we'd not been in touch for ages. Besides Connor wouldn't ever call me a sexy bitch, babe was more his style, so sadly I didn't think they'd be from him either.

I briefly ran through the (longish) list of names of men who I'd been on dates with but quickly discounted them all. Besides, none of them had my address. I was genuinely puzzled. Picking up my phone I snapped a picture of the flowers and messaged it to Jill -

Look what I got!

Wow! Totally OTT but niiiice!
Ben? X

Not Ben x

??! Who then?

Haven't a bloody clue!

Ooh you have a secret
admirer x

It would appear so but it was a mystery that I could have done without having to puzzle over that particular day.

The next day, Friday - Mad Paddy's regular karaoke night at the pub. I met Jill and Becky for a vodka or two and maybe a spot of abusing the other patrons ears with my awful singing. We had been there about an hour when scary Tanya showed up looking even scarier than usual, she was obviously livid about something. Her pissed off-ness was coming off her in waves. People were moving out of her way in alarm as if she was a growling, hungry lioness that had escaped from the zoo as she stomped through the pub. I briefly considered suggesting hiding in the loo but too late, she spotted us and made her way over to where we were standing at the bar.

"Thought you lot might be in here" she said slamming a designer handbag that probably cost more than I earned in a month into a puddle of beer on the bar with a thud.

We mumbled our hello's carefully, none of us daring to ask her what was wrong in case we invited her wrath. She banged her hand on the bar demanding service from Dominic the barman who came scurrying over immediately to do her bidding. Ordering four Sambucas but not to share, we all watched open-mouthed as she downed them all herself one after another then ordered a double Gin.

"Mark's left me" she announced matter of factly, after downing the shots, explaining her darker than usual mood. Lifting her gin glass towards us she shouted "Cheers!" and then necked it in one.

"What?!" I said, shocked "Really, why?"

"Because he's a dickless fucking wanking dickhead with no bollocks"

I tried to get my head around that as she continued "He's ran off with his fat secretary. I mean what a fucking clichè, his sodding secretary for fuck's sake! Never had any fucking imagination that wanker!"

We all looked at her still open-mouthed, not knowing what to say. "You look like a bunch of pissing goldfish" she growled "stop gawping at me like that!"

"Sorry" said Jill "it's just such a shock. Are you OK? I mean, obviously you're not OK but, wow! When did this happen?"

"Got home today to find he'd cleared out all his stuff whilst I was at work. He'd left me a note on the kitchen counter. He wants a divorce. The fucking coward couldn't even tell me face to face! Seventeen years of marriage and he leaves me a pissing note. The bastard."

To be fair, in Mark's position I would have left a note too. In fact I think I would have fled the country and sent a letter. Even in a good mood Tanya was the scariest person I knew. In a bad mood, especially if it was you that was the cause of that bad mood, it was debatable whether you would survive the ensuing onslaught.

"Have you spoken to him?" asked Becky

"Nope, he won't answer my calls, the cowardly fucker"

So that was our Friday night out well and truly buggered up. Tanya got completely mortal on gin and Sambuca, shouted along to "I Will Survive! " on the karaoke then passed out in a chair. It was bloody hard work getting her into a taxi and getting her home. We all knew the taxi driver, Andy, he picked us up on a regular basis and was used to our varying degrees of drunkenness which was the only reason he agreed to take her after getting a promise out of us that if she threw up or pissed in the taxi we would pay for cleaning. We debated between ourselves whether one of us should go with her but none of us were brave enough. "She'll be OK with Andy" said Jill as we watched the taxi drive off with her.

"Yes, but will Andy be OK with her?" asked Becky

"He's a big strong chap, he'll be fine." I said but I wasn't so sure about that.

CHAPTER SIX

After the disastrous Friday night no one was going out that Saturday, we were all in hiding from super angry Tanya, so I had a nice relaxing evening soaking in the bath, listening to music, and as I was seeing Ben the following evening, making sure my lady garden was neatly groomed and checking that I had no stray nipple or chin hairs. What are they all about? I mean, you look at your nips one day and they're perfectly hair free. Look the next day and there'a a six inch straggler which has literally grown overnight! No other hair grows that fast. Ben had asked if I fancied going to the swinger's club again with him and I'd said yes straight away. I'd enjoyed our first encounter there and I'd also enjoyed the uninhibited way it had made me feel. I didn't have any urges to 'play' with any of the other people that were there but being almost naked in front of a bunch of strangers felt good. Maybe I was an exhibitionist and I just hadn't realised it yet.

Happy that I was stray hair free I continued my rock n roll Saturday night and had just settled in bed with a cup of tea and a book I'd been meaning to read for months when Ben video called me. We chatted for a while about what we had been doing that day and I brought him up to date on the Tanya and Mark situation, not that he knew either of them, he'd yet to meet any of my friends. It was really hard to concentrate on the conversation because seeing him and hearing his voice was making me feel more than a little randy. I told him this and he grinned at me, "What are you wearing?" he asked

"Oh, just this, as you can see, it's not very sexy." I replied tilting my phone so he could see my embarrassingly scruffy, old, once white now washed out grey, too big cheap fleece dressing gown. I really did need to invest in a new one.

"You'd look sexy in anything." he said "Have you anything on underneath?"

"No"

"Show me." He demanded

I took off my dressing gown a little reluctantly and quickly showed him my seen better days, but clean, exfoliated, hair free, and recently lotioned body, whilst, without making it too obvious, trying to stop my tits from disappearing under my armpits.

"Mmmm. Nice. Now, masterbate for me." He demanded.

Do what?! My face flamed. "Er, I don't think I can

do that!" I stuttered

"Why not?"

Why not? I didn't know, because I didn't want to? Actually, I did want to, the very idea was turning me on even more. Fuck it, I decided, I was going to do it.

Placing my phone on its stand on my bedside table and turning it so he could watch. I started to pleasure myself. I felt shy and self conscious at first knowing Ben was watching but I soon relaxed and got into the rhythm finding the idea that he was watching me was making me very horny indeed. I soon climaxed and looked at him feeling shy and a little dirty once I got my breath back. He was watching me intently, an unfathomable expression on his face. "You're a bad girl" he told me "You're getting twelve of my belt next time."

Oh God the fanny flutters! Normally someone calling me a bad girl would have me rolling my eyes and laughing but not Ben, him calling me a bad girl and telling me I was getting the belt made me horny as hell.

The next night, Sunday I was practically fizzing with lust and excitement whilst I was waiting for Ben to pick me up to go to the club. He arrived right on time at seven. I opened the door and he kissed me, then held my hand and led me to his car opening the door for me, acting like the perfect gentleman. The nosy old mare across the road was peeking around her flowery curtains so I gave her a cheeky wave and blew her a kiss as we drove off. We went for a quick bite to eat and arrived at the club around nine. There were a lot of people already there that evening and it was quite a squeeze in the bubbling jacuzzi which was lovely and hot. Someone had gone a bit mental with the chlorine and there were a few red streaming eyes going on. A few people got out after five minutes or so leaving just me, Ben and two other couples in there. I was the only one wearing anything, a black bikini, everyone else had it all hanging out. We all chatted for a while, just ordinary people, strangers naked in a jacuzzi on a Sunday evening discussing the news and the weather as you do. Then, without warning, the two women started kissing each other and having a right good feel of each other's boobs. Right in front of me. I didn't know where to look. I looked at Ben desperately trying to communicate to him that I would like to escape but he was totally distracted by the women watching them intently with his tongue hanging out. I gave his leg a quick nudge under the water, he looked at me with a strange smile on his face "Does that turn you on?" He whispered.

"Not really." I replied. I mean fair play to them, we were in a swinger's club after all but them getting off in such close proximity to me just made me feel a little uncomfortable. And watching Ben's reaction, if I'm going to be honest awoke the little green eyed monster in me.

The two women finally stopped mauling each other, removed their tongues from each other's throats and then thankfully got up and left the Jacuzzi with their other halves, going upstairs to play some more no doubt. Ben looked at me raising his eyebrows "Shall we go upstairs?" he asked.

I knew why he wanted to go upstairs, he wanted to carry on watching the proceedings, maybe even try to join in but I didn't, I wasn't ready for all that yet. Didn't know if I ever would be, I was new to this and hadn't yet figured out if it was my thing. And I wanted Ben all to myself for now, I was still getting to know him. I mean we'd agreed on an open relationship, I knew he was seeing someone else and I was perfectly OK with that but when he was with me, I wanted him to be with only me. The thought of actually watching him with another woman turned my stomach. I wasn't sure how to articulate all this to him though and I was frightened to death of scaring him away so early in the game.

"I'd rather just chill here for a little while longer if it's OK with you?" I said

"Of course it is. I'm sorry, I keep forgetting you're new to all this. There's no rush to get involved, just if and when you're ready." he said, grabbing my hand and squeezing it then kissing me.

I was relieved and smiled at him. "I just want to get to know you better first before maybe getting into anything that involves other people. And I need to figure out if it's for me."

"I want to get to know you better too beautiful and am looking forward very much to doing so. If you decide it's not for you then no pressure, we don't have to go there. There's plenty of other ways we can have fun"

He said that sincerely but I had a strong suspicion that he really did want me to get onboard with the swinging at some point. We had a pleasurable rest of the evening at the club, finishing up with some energetic, sweaty sex in one of the tiny private rooms with the red pvc covered bed and the mirrored walls. I still couldn't believe what an excellent lover he was but obviously he'd had lots of practice over the years and was very skilled in his craft. He drove me home much later, me sitting in his car lost in a post multiple orgasm glow, grinning like a simpleton and glad I wasn't driving because I was finding it very hard to concentrate due to the sex flashbacks I was experiencing. When we arrived back at my house he got out of the car, retrieved a black carrier bag from the back seat and walked me up the path. After kissing me gently at the door and giving me a long hug he handed me the bag. "I'll see you on Wednesday" he said, "and you will be wearing this for me. Good night gorgeous creature, sleep well."

I took the bag off him "Good night" I replied and watched him walk back down the path to his car. Once he'd driven away I went inside, turned on the light and looked inside the bag. There was something wrapped in tissue paper. I took it out and unwrapped it to find a black leather collar and a note.

When you wear this for me it means you're submitting to me and you're mine to do with as I please.

I put the collar around my neck, snapped shut the press studs and looked at myself in the mirror. Sexy bitch I thought.

CHAPTER SEVEN

Time dragged so slowly for the next few days but Wednesday finally came around. Did I want to wear the collar? Did I want to submit to him? I thought about little else. I must admit the idea excited me but I hardly knew him, was this something I really wanted to explore with him so early in our relationship? He had suggested booking a hotel room again but, although he insisted it was fine and he could afford it, I felt guilty about him spending money on hotels when he could just come to my house. He knew where I lived now so what difference would it make? I changed the bed sheets, and as I was so full of pent up sexual energy to sit still for even a minute cleaned the whole house from top to bottom. Once I had done that, showered, put on my make up and dried my hair I still had thirty minutes to kill. Time is such a strange thing, if I'd have been going to a meeting or on a night out with the girls the time would have flown by and I would have been running late. Because I was counting the minutes until Ben arrived they were going so frustratingly slowly. I was too excited to sit still and wandered around my tiny house straightening things that didn't need it and moving stuff about only to put it back in its original place five minutes later. At least while I was pacing around the house I was clocking up my steps. I thought I might even make the previously unattainable 10,000 if he was later than I was expecting him. What, with all this pacing around and all this sexercise I'd be burning off loads of calories which meant I would be shifting a few pounds that I definitely could afford to lose. Win win. I went into my bedroom to check there was nothing out of place for the hundredth time and took the collar from my bedside drawer where it had been since Ben had given it to me on Sunday. I was still unsure about it. I'd tried it on a few times, I liked how it felt around my neck, it made me feel sexy and even though wearing it meant I would be submitting to him the idea made me feel strangely powerful and desirable.

Ben arrived right on time. I glanced at my smart watch, 9,637 steps, so near yet so far! We hugged for a moment and he kissed me. He smelt so good. We had a cup of tea and chatted for a little while on the sofa before going up to my bedroom, well I didn't want to look like a complete harlot by dragging him straight upstairs as soon as he walked in the door.

"Are you going to wear the collar?" he asked

when we got to my bedroom.

I made my decision "Yes" I told him.

"Good girl."

I took off my old dressing gown to reveal a black lace all in one and hold up stockings of course. From scruff to sexy in two seconds. He smiled his approval at what I was wearing. Taking the collar from my bedside table drawer I fastened it snugly around my neck.

"Not too tight" he said, reaching around me, lifting my hair and loosening the collar a little. "That's better, we don't want you choking. Now remember, by wearing that you are agreeing to do exactly what I tell you."

I swallowed, and nodded at him, feeling nervous and excited all at once, my stomach doing backflips. I was shaking slightly as I waited for him to tell me what he wanted me to do.

"Get on your knees" he ordered

That again! Good grief. My knees protested loudly as I got down, popping like a couple of firecrackers going off.

"Look at me," he said.

I did as I was told, lifting my head and looking up into his face. He held my gaze for a while then grabbed my hair pulling it tightly up on top of my head in his fist. "You are beautiful," he told me, his voice gruff.

Compliments embarrass me and I automatically opened my mouth to disagree but he put his free hand over my mouth and shook his head. "No talking"

He let go of my hair and helped me back onto my feet, telling me to turn and face the wall and to put my hands flat on the wall above my head. He leaned his body against me pushing my breasts up against the hard surface, I could feel the cold through the thin lace of my bodysuit. Wrapping my hair in his fist again, holding it out of the way he started to lightly bite my neck, shoulders and earlobes. Oh that felt sooo good, I felt weak at the knees, groaned out loud and was shivering with delight. He was still fully dressed but I could feel his erection pushing against the bottom of my back through his jeans. He let go of my hair and stopped with the neck biting after a couple of minutes. Telling me not to move he pulled away from me slightly and undid his belt. I heard the slight clink of the buckle as he unfastened it then the sound of the leather belt sliding through the loops of his jeans as he pulled it free.

"You know what's coming next. You're getting twelve today" he told me.

I did get twelve in two lots of six, him rubbing my bum cheeks in between and I enjoyed every single one of them. They were not too hard but hard enough for my arse to be stinging a little after he'd finished.

"Was that OK?" he asked.

"Yes." I told him.

Again he caressed and rubbed my bum cheeks after he'd finished with the belt then he took the collar off my neck. I felt a little disappointed as I took it from him and put it back in my drawer, I was enjoying being submissive.

"There's much, much more to come" he promised "but I want to take it slowly, build up your trust."

He began to kiss me and then made sweet, gentle love to me in complete contrast to the bossy man he had been just five minutes earlier, holding me tightly and telling me how beautiful I was.

We snoozed for a short while afterwards wrapped up in each other's arms but just before midnight he got up, showered, got dressed and left, leaving me feeling disappointed once again. The bubble of fantasy I'd been happily living in for the last few hours popped and I was brought rudely back to reality. I had a word with myself. It's just sex, remember, just sex. It was a long, long time before I fell asleep again.

CHAPTER EIGHT

The next day a loud knocking at the door woke me up. Groaning, I tried to focus my eyes so I could see the time on my phone, 7am. Who the hell was banging on my door at this ungodly hour?! I got up, shrugged on my dressing gown and staggered downstairs half asleep to find a delivery man who was far too cheerful for his own good, especially so early in the feckin morning. He was holding a small cardboard box. I looked at him puzzled, I hadn't ordered anything, it was probably for one of the neighbours. Number 21 had a real love affair going on with online shopping and I took so many parcels in for him it was ridiculous. I felt annoyed at being woken so early to take yet another parcel in for my neighbour but when I looked at the label, it wasn't for Craig at number 21 it actually had my name and address on for a change. I took the box and mumbled my grumpy thanks to Mr Insanely Happy who told me it was "No problemo!" and ordered me to have a nice day with a big white toothy smile and a wink. I turned to go inside then stopped, the hairs prickled at the back of my neck, it felt like someone was watching me. I looked back at the delivery man but he was already putting his van in gear and driving away still wearing his insane grin, (he was definitely medicated no one is naturally that happy). I looked across the road at Nosy Nancy's flowery curtained bay window but there was no sign of her for a change. I looked up and down the street but I couldn't see anyone. Strange. I felt a shiver down my spine and shuddered. Going back inside I quickly, closed and locked the door behind me. Once I was in the living room I shook the box, feeling a bit reluctant to open it in case it contained something horrible. "Oh get a sodding grip!" I told myself, I really needed to stop watching so many horror films. I opened the box to find nothing sinister, just a cute stuffed brown toy dog with big glittery blue eyes and a red heart shaped nose looking at me. There was a card inside, a hearts and flowers romantic effort with two words written inside. ***Sexy bitch.*** Must have been from the same person that sent me the flowers. Puzzled, I sat the toy on the table, snapped a pic and sent it to Jill with a question mark. My phone pinged straight back. Unlike me, Jill is a morning person and I knew she'd be awake -

Another gift from your

secret admirer?

Yeah. Not a bloody clue who it's off!

Ooh, exciting x

A bit scary more like x

I went to the kitchen to make myself a coffee but when I checked the jar I had none left. Bloody hell, I couldn't function without a strong dose of caffeine in the morning. I decided to get dressed and go to Penny's, the local bakery / cafe for breakfast, do a bit of work there, the change of scenery would do me good. I shoved an old track-suit on, put my hair up in a messy bun, brushed my teeth and gave my face a quick wash. Briefly considered a bit of makeup but decided I really couldn't be bothered.

Penny's was fairly busy when I got there but most of the early morning crowd had gone off to work so there were a couple of tables free. As I walked towards the back of the room towards an empty one I noticed a familiar face sitting at the table next to it. It was Mark, Tanya's (soon to be ex) husband. He was sitting with a chubby lady with dark curly hair and a lovely, pretty face. I wondered briefly if I should leave but it was too late, he'd spotted me. "Oh, hi Scarlett. How lovely to see you." He said smiling warmly at me. He looked relaxed and happy which wasn't how I was used to seeing him, he had always looked harassed and stressed on the few occasions had seen him with Tanya.

"Good morning" I replied, smiling back at him and the mystery lady who was also smiling. Polite smiles all round.

"This is Jane, my secretary, Jane, this is Scarlett, she's a friend of Tanya's." Mark said introducing us.

"Good morning, Scarlett, pleased to meet you." said Jane standing up and reaching out to shake my hand. I don't think hand shaking came naturally to Jane, I suspected she was more of a hugger like Shona but she probably thought hugging a friend of Tanya's was inappropriate.

"Pleased to meet you too." I said, letting go of her soft, warm hand after more of a squeeze than a shake. I considered asking Mark how he was but it was all a little awkward so I decided against making further conversation "Well, I'll leave you to it, enjoy your breakfast." I said, still smiling at them. My cheeks were beginning to ache.

"Bye, have a lovely day." replied Mark. That was like three whole sentences, it was the most words I had ever heard him speak in one go. Giving them a little nod I turned away and made my way towards a different table than I had originally intended, one a little further away. Sitting down I wondered if Jane was who Mark had left Tanya for, if so you certainly couldn't have got much different. Physically they were complete opposites, Tanya being tall, blonde, very slim, very well groomed with her designer clothes and perfect hair and nails. Jane was short and plump with no makeup to speak of and neat but plain clothes that were more Primark than Armani. Jane came across as very warm and friendly whereas Tanya was quite hard, all sharp edges with an abrupt nature. In all honesty I couldn't blame Mark for leaving her but I couldn't say that to him, I had to show solidarity to my friend I suppose even if I didn't really like her all that much.

I got my head down and managed to get a couple of hours work done with the help of four cups of strong black coffee and a naughty but nice Danish pastry, leaving the cafe around quarter to twelve before it started to get busy with the lunchtime crowd. Arriving home I suddenly got a case of goosebumps, I had the strangest feeling that someone had been in the house. I put my keys down quietly on the coffee table and stood really still listening for a while. I didn't hear anything unusual, just the normal muted sounds of life going on outside. Traffic and bird song mostly. I checked all five rooms and even under the bed but there was no one there. I shook my head at myself "I'm going mad!" I said with a nervous laugh to the cat who had wandered into the bedroom behind me and was looking at me suspiciously. He agreed with me, he already thought I was completely mental anyway. Getting up off the bedroom floor I noticed the toy dog on my pillow. Puzzled, I looked at it for a moment then picked it up and shoved it in the wardrobe. I was sure I had left it on the coffee table before I went to the cafe.

That evening I had a dinner date round at my neighbour Alfie's. I had been looking forward to it for days, he was an excellent chef, a skill he had shamelessly admitted to perfecting with the sole intention of using it to impress the ladies. He was a real ladies man, but a real gentleman with it. He had recently returned from a cruise, one of the many holidays he took every year. A widowed, retired dentist in his late seventies Alfie was still very good looking, fit and healthy, he was great company, a complete extrovert and an outrageous flirt. I'd missed him whilst he'd been away. He wanted to know all about my summer fling with his house guest Connor.

"I believe you got on very well indeed with Connor." He said as we sat sipping wine after a delicious homemade lasagna, garlic bread and a generous slice of lemon drizzle cake also homemade. Carb overload, would probably be four pounds heavier in the morning but it was well worth it.

I felt my face flush. "Oh, I do believe she is blushing!" said Alfie, teasing me a little.

I laughed "He was a very nice person, we had a very nice time."

"Mmmm, a *very* nice time. Very easy on the eye too, I'm led to believe. How was he in bed? Excellent I am guessing!"

"Alfie!" I scolded him pretending to be insulted.

"A lady never tells."

"Good job you're not a lady then isn't it? The village is rife with gossip about you, you are providing all the natter at the knit and natter group."

"Oh God." I said putting my free hand over my face feeling a little embarrassed.

"Ah don't worry yourself about it. The old dears pretend to be outraged when really they're all insanely jealous of you. Their vaginas dried up a long time ago, they have to live their sex lives vicariously through gorgeous girls such as yourself. So spill, how was the sex?!"

"It was excellent. He was a sexy guy, gorgeous and fun, and great company."

"Well, you're very welcome." He said smiling "I will try to accommodate you with more sexy house guests in the future."

"Thank you. If they're as sexy as Connor I will happily look after them for you. Although, I'm actually seeing someone at the moment." I told him

"What? As in seriously? As in you've been on more than two dates with him?"

"Oh, har har! Yes, more than two dates. It's a little complicated though."

"Isn't it always. Go on, tell me."

I told him about Ben, how we'd met and about his living arrangement with Gina.

"Sounds like a whole load of bullshit to me." said Alfie in his usual no nonsense manner "I predict heartbreak with this one Scarlett, be on your guard with him."

"Oh, don't worry it's just a sex thing." I assured him

"I think, you're kidding yourself. You like him, more than you're willing to admit. I can tell by the way you talk about him. You smile when you say his name. Your face lights up. You're falling for him. Watch yourself, guard your feelings or you're going to get hurt. I don't like him."

"You never like any of the men I date" I pointed out "and you don't even know him, how can you decide if you like him or not if you've never even met him?"

"I might be getting a little long in the tooth now but I'm still a man, I know how they think. Look how right I've been before about the men you've dated." He did have a point there. It had, after all, never worked out with any of them "I just don't like what you're telling me about him, something is off. Mark my words, that man isn't quite what he seems. Don't let your feelings blind you to what he really is."

CHAPTER NINE

Ben and I continued to see each other a couple of times a week exploring a mild sub / dom relationship most of the time but other times just having very excellent, satisfying sex. I really looked forward to our time together and continued to be disappointed when he left me afterwards which he invariably did. I questioned him asking why he couldn't stay over and he explained to me that he had to be at home in case Gina took ill. He stayed away from home with work on a regular basis, sometimes several hours drive away and that didn't seem to cause a problem, but he couldn't stay with me for some reason. I argued that he had his phone and he could be back home within half an hour if she called him but he was adamant that he couldn't spend the night with me and as I'd agreed to the boundaries of our relationship I felt I had no right to ask more of him but the fuck and run nature of the relationship was beginning to piss me off somewhat. My feelings were confusing me. I'd had friends with benefits relationships before that were based solely on sex and where I'd never stayed overnight with them and that hadn't bothered me at all but I felt differently about Ben. I began to question his relationship with Gina, was what he told me the truth? My gut instincts were telling me he wasn't being totally honest with me but I didn't want to lose him so didn't want to confront him about it. To be honest I hate confrontation, I'm a little fearful of it and I am terrible at dealing with things head on in a rational way and would much rather just let things piss me off until I explode, usually when I've had a little too much to drink. I've fucked things up quite often with this approach but I was still guilty of doing it. Maybe, one day I would learn, or even find a man that understood me. Stranger things have happened.

I came to the conclusion that I was getting far too emotionally involved with Ben, he was taking up too much headspace. I was finding it hard to concentrate on work or anything that didn't involve him. That wasn't good so I decided perhaps it was time to take a step back. Take some space to deal with what was fast becoming an infatuation. Perhaps I should date other people, we were in an open, sex only relationship after all and I knew that he was seeing at least one other person as well as me.

I was home alone one evening and bored so I decided to pop back on the dating sites to see what was on offer. I still had profiles on three sites but I had hidden them a few weeks earlier because I was happy just seeing Ben. After trudging through what felt like a thousand unsuitable profiles I finally arranged a date with a good looking guy called David. It was a bit of a strange one to say the least.

We met at a little cafe in a neighbouring town. I didn't recognise him at first, mostly because he was clean shaven and traditionally dressed in his photos but he now happened to be sporting a big unruly bushy beard and matching eyebrows. He was wearing a strange, long, multi-coloured robe of some sort and was sitting barefoot and cross legged on a settee with his eyes closed humming to himself when I walked into the cafe. Looking at him briefly, slightly amused by his eccentricities, not realising he was my date and thinking he hadn't arrived yet I got myself a drink and sat at a table to wait for him. A few minutes later he walked over to me. "Scarlett, autumnal beauty of the woods." he announced in a loud voice as he approached my table. He put his hands together and bowed his head as in prayer "Namaste"

"Oh, Erm, hello. David?" I replied bemused.

"Yes, that is my given name but I prefer my spiritual name Bodhi, he of the enlightened soul. It was given to me by the Reiki master who cured then taught me. May I sit sweet lady?" he enquired, indicating the chair opposite mine.

"Of course." I said, thinking bloody hell, what a

nutter, get me out of here!

He stared at me studying my face intently for a few awkward moments, I opened my mouth and started to ask him a question just to break the silence but he held his hand up, palm towards me and gently shushed me. His eyes were now focused on a spot just above my head and he appeared to be deep in concentration.

Standing back up, shaking his head, he walked behind my chair and stood behind me with his hand just above my head. "You have a beautiful aura but your chakra is in turmoil, lady of the woods, I fear you partake a little too much in the consumption of alcohol. Allow me to try to restore it back to health." OK yes I enjoyed a drink or three, sometimes a bit too much, but how did he know this? He took a small wooden stick with tiny silver bells on it from what I'm guessing was a pocket hidden somewhere in his colourful robes along with a small purple crystal which he gave to me. "Amethyst, yours to keep to guard you against intoxication."

Was this some kind of wind up I thought, taking the crystal which was smooth, cold and hard in my hand. I searched the faces of the other customers in the cafe who were watching the proceedings with amusement to see if there was anyone there I knew. Had my friends put him up to this? Did somebody have a camera? Was it some kind of YouTube stunt? He started to hum loudly again and do some strange shit with his hands wafting them around my head and shoulders whilst intermittently shaking the tiny silver bells over me. By this point some of the other customers were openly laughing. I shrugged my shoulders at an elderly man who was watching us over his newspaper and mouthed "First date. Help!" he just smiled at me and shook his head, no help at all. Thanks mate.

"I did my best sweet one." David / Bodhi said sitting back down after a few minutes of this weirdness, I think you will need some more sessions to balance things properly and find your peace with the world once more. His hand disappeared into his robes once more reappearing with a white business card which he handed over to me. Bodhi - Reiki Master & Spiritual Healer was printed in curly script across it with a picture of praying hands and his phone number. Using the dating sites to drum up business, fair play to him I suppose, even the spiritually enlightened amongst us needed to eat.

Thankfully my next date was of the normal variety. He was called Neil, his face was familiar but that was probably because he lived quite close to me. A little too close for comfort if I'm to be honest I would usually make sure there was at least a fifteen minute drive between me and potential shag buddies so that it was unlikely we would bump into each other if and when we fell out or in case he had stalkerish tendencies but Neil lived in the same village and I think I'd spied him in the pub on occasion. The pickings were rather slim among the potentially sane, solvent, single, reasonably good looking men in my age group within a twenty mile radius and I'd already dated half of them so beggars couldn't be choosers. I reasoned I could always just blank him if need be, pretend I didn't know him if things turned into a total disaster.

When we met for coffee one lunchtime at Penny's I was pleasantly surprised, he appeared normal and he actually looked like his picture. In fact he was better looking in real life which was a rarity. He was tall, around about the 6'2" he had claimed to be instead of the usual 5'7" and five or six inches of imagination. He was just the right amount of chunky for me, I like something to cuddle up to, with reddish hair and a neat beard framing a strong jawline.

"Hiya, Neil?" I asked approaching him in the busy cafe.

"Hello, Scarlett." he said smiling at me and standing up "Sit down, what can I get you?"

"It's OK, I'll go." I said, indicating his half empty cup "Do you want another?"

"No, I'll go, sit down and do as you're told!" He laughed and winked at me. Mmm, a forceful guy, I liked that.

"OK, thanks, if you insist. Just an Americano for me please, black, no sugar." I took off my jacket, hung it on the back of my chair and sat down.

"Shouldn't forget that, same as I drink. Back in a tick." What a coincidence. Most people these days tend to drink the more fashionable lattes or cappuccinos or mochaccino or whatever. Me, I just like a no-nonsense strong dose of caffeine, straight up. Although I did once have a bit of a love affair with iced frappes for a while until Jill made me wise to their ridiculously high calorie and sugar content.

Neil went to the counter to order the coffees, giving me the chance to admire his excellent arse which was nicely encased in indigo jeans. Turning round, he caught me checking him out and grinned at me. "Would you like anything else? Cake perhaps? Or maybe a bun?" he asked, teasing me.

"No thanks" I replied, blushing a little.

He was soon back with the coffees. "You go in the Hare and Hounds don't you? I've heard you singing on the karaoke there on a Friday once or twice."

Oh god, the shame. "Er, yeah. I apologise for any damage caused to your ears!"

He laughed "Ah, you're not that bad. Not as bad as Sharon. Her singing curdles the beer." We both laughed at this, Sharon was so bad at karaoke she was a legend. Completely tone deaf and no idea of timing whatsoever, she was so bad it was actually genius, everyone loved her. "To be honest, I've always fancied you a bit. Thought you were coupled up though that's why I never said anything to you in the pub. Was happily surprised to see you were on Tinder." Neil told me.

"No, I'm single." Was I? Kind of. I considered my relationship with Ben. For all intents and purposes I guess I was.

We chatted for an hour or so in the cafe getting along really well with one another. In addition to liking the same type of coffee we discovered we had quite a lot of other things in common too. We both liked whiskey, enjoyed the same types of food a bit too much, tried to avoid eating too many carbs as they made us gain weight but gave in to the temptation of pizza once in a while. We had the same taste in music and would rather read a good book than watch mindless drivel on the TV. We'd both rather go for a long walk than work out in the gym, liked to travel a lot and had many of the same places on our travel wish-lists. He made me laugh and I found him very attractive.

Sadly, all too soon Neil had to leave because he was on his lunch break and had to go back to work but before we parted we made arrangements for me to go round to his house, which was only a few minutes from mine, the following evening to watch a film and try a drop or two from his whiskey collection.

I called round to Neils the next night as arranged and was surprised at his pleasant, neat little home. It had none of the usual stereotypical single male monotone decor, too-big telly, games consoles, black leather settee etc. It was modern but cosy, very clean and tidy. All soft yellows, lilacs and greys. We had a very pleasant evening, getting to know each other a little better, half watching some macho film with not much of a story line but plenty of swearing, swaggering, fighting, shooting and car chases whilst sampling some very nice whiskey and treating ourselves to a naughty pizza. We rounded the night off with a little bit of tipsy snogging and I got a taxi home after we made arrangements to see each other again in the pub a few days later. I didn't think about Ben once.

When I arrived home, feeling content and warm inside from the whiskey and the excellent company, I discovered a white carrier bag sitting on my doorstep. Written on the side of the bag in black marker and large letters was, you guessed it, ***sexy bitch***. I looked around but I couldn't see anyone. Approaching the bag warily I peeked inside. There was a bottle of my favourite wine, a single red rose and a box of Black Magic. What the hell? This had to be someone who knew me fairly well, well enough to know what wine and chocolates I liked at least. I picked the bag up, took it around the side of the house and threw it straight into the bin. I hated to waste the wine and chocolates but I didn't want them, what if they were poisoned? I have a wild imagination I know but it wasn't beyond the realms of possibility. This was getting way beyond weird.

The next morning, I wandered downstairs half asleep for my caffeine fix. On my way to the kitchen I noticed a note behind the door. I picked it up and read the message - ***ungrateful bitch*** was scrawled in untidy writing on a page that had been ripped from a pocket diary. I shuddered, whoever had left the bag must have been watching me last night and seen me throw it in the bin. I was beginning to get scared. I made a coffee and debated calling the police. And say what? That someone keeps sending me gifts. I think I may be being watched. I could imagine them down at the police station, rolling their eyes and laughing at the silly single woman overreacting, looking for attention, patronising me, thinking Jesus does she not think we've got enough real crime to investigate? I decided to call Jill instead and ask her advice about the bag.

"You need to call the police." She said without preamble "It's bloody weird, and it's getting bloody scary. Have you no idea at all who it may be?"

"Not the foggiest." I replied. I honestly didn't have a clue.

I felt a bit stupid but I did what she told me and phoned the police. I was surprised when they took me seriously telling me they would send an officer round to see me later that day. Around 4pm there was a knock at the door, I opened it to find two female police officers who showed me their warrant cards and introduced themselves as PC Steph Walker and PC Jenny Smith. I invited them into the house and began to explain to them what had been happening, starting with the flowers. "I feel a bit silly" I admitted as I told them about the gifts and showed them the note "and I hope you don't think that I am overreacting but it's actually starting to scare me a little bit, especially knowing someone was probably watching me last night."

"Don't feel silly" said PC Smith "If it's worrying you then we're happy to look into it for you. Do you still have the items?" I no longer had the flowers they had long since died, but I showed her the picture I had sent to Jill. The police officer whistled when she looked at the picture "Wow! That's some bouquet, must have cost a fortune."

Next I showed them the toy dog and explained how it had moved and how sure I was that it wasn't me that had moved it "Do you still have the box it came in and the card?" asked PC Smith. I did and I went to fetch them from the kitchen. "Is it OK if we take this?" she asked putting the dog back into the box it had come in.

"Yes, of course" I said

"We'll see if we can get any fingerprints or anything off it and return it to you."

"It's OK, I don't really want it back."

"Does anyone else have keys to your house?" asked PC Walker

"Only my daughter and my friend Jill"

"And there's been no signs of any break ins?"

"No"

"OK, well check that your daughter and your friend have still got your key and haven't given it to anyone else or lost it."

We went outside to the bin to retrieve the bag I had thrown away the night before. Opening the lid I looked inside to find it had gone. A little flustered I looked at the two police officers, "I definitely put it in there." I said "He must have taken it out again."

"Don't worry. Just describe the bag and contents." said PC Smith

I did as I was asked and she wrote the description in her note book. "OK", she said, snapping the book shut "We'll be in touch soon. Let us know if anything else happens and if you think there's someone in your home or you feel in danger at any time don't hesitate to ring 999. It's what we're here for."

I thanked them for their time and they left. I noticed Nosy Nancy across the road peering through her pristine net curtains no doubt besides herself with curiosity. The woman had never said two words to me since I moved in yet she probably knew more about my life than anyone else. Perhaps the police should go and have a chat with her I thought. I gave her a little wave and went back inside.

CHAPTER TEN

The following Sunday Ben and I went for a meal. I hadn't seen him all week as he had been working away and even though I'd had a couple of very enjoyable dates with Neil I had missed him. At the restaurant he was preoccupied with his phone and I was starting to get a bit annoyed with the ignorant arse. I picked up my own phone and messaged him to get his attention.

Hello! Can we be in the room please!
Be nice to have a conversation!!!

He read my message and looked up at me. "So sorry babe, I was just answering some messages."

"Can't they wait?" I asked, sticking out my bottom lip and pretending to sulk.

He laughed at me "Of course, sorry that was rude of me." He put his phone on the table and I glanced at it wondering what the messages were and why they were so important they couldn't wait. The screen went black but not before I could see the website he'd been on - Swopportunities - the swingers site. I felt a mixture of annoyance and jealousy, but I could hardly say anything as I had agreed to an open relationship and I had been on other dates. I needed to get a grip, it was just sex, he wasn't my boyfriend, just my friend with benefits. But still, I was upset and I didn't enjoy the meal, not eating much because of the knot of anxiety in my stomach.

We went back to my house after the meal, the sex was amazing as always but I wasn't really feeling it that night. My mind was full of images of Ben with other women and it was making me burn with jealousy. Try as I might I just couldn't get the thoughts out of my head. He picked up on my mood and asked me what was wrong. "Nothing" I lied. How could I tell him how I was feeling when I had readily agreed to the rules of our open relationship. The truth was I was beginning to regret agreeing to those rules. I realised what I was beginning to feel for Ben was much more than just friends with benefits allowed but he had been clear from the start that it couldn't be anything more. My other friends with benefits relationships had been fine, I'd easily kept within the boundaries and not developed feelings for either of them but with Ben it was different. I was falling for him. This wasn't good. He didn't help matters with his hugs and kisses and ringing me everyday calling me beautiful - surely that wasn't in the friends with benefits rule book?

After he left, just before midnight as usual, I

lay, wide awake, staring at the ceiling. My mind was working overtime. What should I do? I didn't want to lose him, a little bit of something wonderful was still wonderful but I didn't think I could cope with the jealousy I was feeling. It was making me miserable. Over and over in my mind I debated - should I end the relationship or should I just accept it for what it was and make the best of it? Finally, still undecided and totally exhausted, I fell asleep.

A couple of days later I got a message off Neil asking if I fancied going to the cinema with him that evening. I wasn't sure what to do, I did really like him and I was getting the impression that he really liked me too but Ben had a hold over me that I just couldn't seem to shake off. Was it fair to keep dating Neil? Should I tell him about Ben? Should I tell Ben about Neil? Both relationships were just casual I reasoned with myself so what harm to see both and keep my options open? I messaged back -

Yes, I'd like that x

We went to the cinema, sneaking in our chocolate, sweets and drinks like we were smuggling heroin into a school. I wasn't really interested in the film to be honest, it was a bit boring, some war thriller thing with Rosamund Pike wearing a weird eye patch for a reason I couldn't fathom out probably because I couldn't be bothered following the story. I did enjoy snuggling up to Neil whilst stuffing my face with the illicit chocolate and sweets though. Everybody knows that the same rules apply as on long car journeys, on holiday, at birthdays,Christmas and Easter, and after relationship breakups and that calories from treats consumed at the cinema don't count so I always eat more sugar in an hour and half there than I normally would in a whole month, not stopping until I felt thoroughly sick. I kept sneaking looks at Neil's profile in the semi-darkness of the auditorium whilst attempting to bring on the diabetes. He really was handsome, his strong, firm jaw, the total opposite to Ben's tired, soft, sagging features. He even had sexy hair, thick and stylishly tousled. Hair you could imagine running your fingers through whilst he made love to you. I wondered what he was like in bed, imagining his firm arms holding me and...oh I was getting so horny. He caught me staring at him and growled "Stop admiring me Red and watch the bloody film. And stop eating all the best Revels!" Then he laughed and kissed my cheek. A woman in front of us with a face like a slapped arse turned and shushed us. Neil blew her a kiss and she turned back round with a loud, disgusted tut setting us both off giggling like a couple of big kids - mostly in silence but with the occasional snort that set her off huffing again.

Neil dropped me off at home around eleven. I think he was hoping for me to invite him in and

I really, really wanted to but my mind was just too full of Ben. I actually found I cared for Neil beyond just sex and I didn't think it would be fair to him to take things any further whilst I was still involved with Ben. I gave him a quick kiss, thanked him for a lovely evening and reluctantly climbed out of the car, leaving him with a puzzled expression on his face. He wound down his window and shouted to me as I walked down the path to my front door "Are you going to buy me a drink at the pub on Friday to make up for eating all the nice Revels and leaving me the coffee ones?" he asked.

"Yeah, OK" I said, giving him a wave "See you then, around eight."

He waved back then drove off with a little toot on his horn.

I was a little distracted as I let myself into the house. Neil was a nice guy, he really didn't deserve being messed about, I should be honest with him and tell him about the situation with Ben. Or end things with Ben and just see Neil, but I didn't think that I could. I felt a little guilty and ashamed about my deceitful behaviour. I put my keys on the table, hung up my coat and headed upstairs telling myself I would ring Neil in the morning and explain the situation to him. I'd be gutted if he didn't want to see me any more but at least he would know all the facts. I got to my bedroom door and stopped, it was closed. I was almost 100% sure I had left it open. I always do because Walter liked to sleep on my bed. Holding my breath I opened the door, my hand flying to my mouth in shock when I saw what was waiting for me. My bed was covered in red rose petals, there were lit candles on each of my bedside tables and my lacy red underwear was laid out on my pillow. Sexy bitch was written in lipstick on my dressing table mirror. I immediately ran out of the house calling Jill in panic on my phone. She answered sleepily "This better be an emergency Scarlett."

I tried to explain to her what had happened but I couldn't breathe with panic and I was babbling nonsense.

"SCARLETT!!!" she shouted "Calm the fuck down. What the hell is going on?"

I took a deep breath, managing to calm the panic a little and told her what I had found. "I'm coming over" she said "I will be there in five minutes, phone the police." She ended the call and I did as I was told and rang the police. They promised they would send someone straight away. I was pacing up and down my garden path with my arms wrapped around myself, shaking with cold and fear and feeling exposed. What if he was watching me, what if he attacked me? As promised Jill was there within minutes, still dressed in her pyjamas with a hoody thrown over the top of them. We went inside the house and she hugged me, I was still shaking "It's OK." she said holding me tight until I managed to get the shaking under control. I showed Jill my bedroom. “This is fucking wierd” she said looking at the petals and candles. We didn’t touch anything, didn’t even blow out the candles, just went downstairs where she made us both a cup of tea and sat with me until the police arrived. They arrived not long afterwards, asked their questions, looked at my bedroom and promised to send a crime scene person round the next day to see if they could find any fingerprints. There was no sign of forced entry which was strange, I was 100% sure I had locked the door on my way out. They advised me to get my locks changed as soon as possible then left. I stayed with Jill that night although I didn’t get much sleep.

A couple of days later I realised my Facebook account had been hacked. A picture of my bedroom as it had been after the break in with the rose petals and the candles had been posted with the caption “Waiting for my lover.” Strange. I went to delete it but screenshot it instead to email to PC Smith then hid it from my timeline but leaving it on my account in case they needed to see it. Then I changed my password.

On Friday at the pub I bought Neil a drink as promised and was telling him about what I had found in the house after he had dropped me off on Tuesday and about the weird gifts I had been getting. He looked concerned, “Perhaps I should volunteer to be your bodyguard?” he said “You can pay me in kind” grinning at me.

The police had sent someone round to look for fingerprints but they weren't holding out much hope of finding anything. I'd spent £90 that I couldn't really afford getting the lock changed on my front door even though the only other people that had keys to the house were Jill, my daughter Emily and my landlord. Jill and Emily still had their keys and I doubted very much that my landlord had popped over from Australia where he lived just to leave me rose petals and candles. Still, as the locksmith pointed out, the lock was very old, would be relatively easy to break and could do with changing anyway.

I had a nice evening at the pub with Neil. I introduced him to Julie and Jill who were both out that night. They gave me the thumbs up of approval when he went to the bar.

"Oh, he's lovely" commented Jill "even though he is a ginger! I do know him vaguely from around the village and in here. We've said hello from time to time."

"He is lovely." agreed Julie "Are you two dating?"

"Not really, well, kind of. Oh I don't know. The idea was if I met someone I really liked I would end things with Ben. I do really like Neil, but I just can't bring myself to end things with Ben, I've got a bit too attached to him."

"So why did you go on a date with Neil if you feel this way about Ben?" asked Becky reasonably.

"I honestly don't know. The thing with Ben is just supposed to be casual and I do want something more, I want to settle down, I'm not getting any younger. But I'm not ready to let him go yet."

"Can you not see yourself settling down with Ben?" asked Jill

"He's told me that can't be on the cards, because his life is just too complicated at the moment."

"Because of his lodger?"

"Yeah."

"Seems a bit odd to me." Said Becky

"I agree." I said

"Look, it's really quite simple. If you like Neil and you want a serious relationship then end it with Ben and make a go of it with him." said Jill.

"I wish it was quite so simple." I sighed.

Neil insisted on getting a taxi together and seeing me home later that night. We arrived at my house and went inside where he mock-swept the entire house holding his hands out making a pretend gun shouting "Clear!" as he checked each room. Being a bit drunk we both found this highly hilarious. I made us both a hot chocolate with a shot of Baileys, topped with squirty cream and we sat on the couch sipping the delicious hot sweetness chatting about who my stalker could possibly be. Walter came stalking in, gave Neil a look of distrust and then stalked back off again with his tail and nose stuck up in the air. "Hey fur face, us gingers should stick together." said Neil as Walter left the room. He shrugged "I don't think your cat likes me."

"Ah, don't worry about it. Don't take it personally, he doesn't like anyone. I don't think he even likes me." I explained

"Then why do you put up with him?" Neil asked

"Because I like him." I said

"You're just far too kind." he said

We finished our hot chocolate. Neil placed his mug on the coffee table and then took mine from me placing it next to his. Turning towards me he held my face in his hands and kissed me gently. "Do you want me to stay Red?" he asked.

I did want him to stay, so badly. I was so horny. But I liked him, a lot, and I didn't want to fuck things up with him just for the sake of a shag. I needed to end things with Ben first before I took things any further with Neil. I wanted it to be so much more than just a sex thing with him.

"I do. Honestly I do. But I can't sleep with you right now."

"Have you got the painters in? It's OK if you have, you can just give me a blow job." I gave him a look. "Joking, joking! Honestly I'm just joking, stop with the evils! If you don't fancy me it's fine, I'll get over it. Might take me a few years of therapy to come to terms with the fact that I'm not as devastatingly attractive as I thought I was but I'll be OK in the end. Don't worry."

I laughed. "It's not that. I do fancy you." I did. I really, really fancied him.

"Oh thank God for that!" he joked "What is it

then? What's the deal? Good Catholic girl, no sex before marriage?"

"Hardly. It's just that things are, well, a little bit complicated right now. I just need some time to sort some stuff out."

He rolled his eyes in mock exasperation. "You bloody wimmen and your complications!"

"Sorry."

He smiled at me. "You take as much time as you need. I can do platonic for now. Don't know how long you'll be able to resist this fine specimen of a man though. And you do realise that all the women in the village are after my body."

"Well, apart from Jill who is a lesbian, I am the youngest woman in the village by about 20 years." I pointed out to him.

"Yeah, but some of those older ladies are right little goers on the sly you know!"

I laughed and he gave me a hug "Guess I'd better get gone then before you succumb to my charm. See ya soon."

He left and I locked the door behind him feeling a little sad. The house suddenly felt empty now he'd gone. We could be great together I thought, if only I can get over this infatuation I had with Ben.

CHAPTER ELEVEN

December rolled around bringing Christmas with it. The year had flown by. I don't know why but I always find Christmas utterly depressing. Maybe it's because it's forced down our throats for weeks and weeks on end, adverts, music, spend, spend, spend and spend some more. Not that I'm religious but it has lost its meaning and magic and become, sadly like so much else in this materialistic world, all about the money. Even before Hallowe'en is done with the shops are forcing the season of goodwill and credit card spending upon us. When I'm Prime Minister I'm making any mention of Christmas before 1st December illegal. There's so much pressure to buy those perfect gifts you can't afford and cook perfect food and go to parties that you don't want to go to and pretend to enjoy the company of people you can't stand and manage to avoid the rest of the year. Then, after all that stress and preparation there was the big day itself and it was always a total anti-climax.

Every year I said I was going away for Christmas and every year I didn't. Bah humbug! Thank god for alcohol.

It was a couple of Saturdays before Christmas and I was going to a party that evening at Shona's, oh joy. Although I loved Shona I think I'd rather stop at home and stick pins in my eyes sometimes than go to one of her dos. You'd be forgiven for thinking that a party at Shona and Jed's would be quite exciting as there were almost always a handful of famous people there from the music industry but I'd soon gotten over being starstruck when I discovered that the majority of them were the biggest, egotistical bores ever. No doubt there'd be awful homemade wine and terrible homemade food with loads of kids running around smearing their sticky mits all over your best frock and trying to climb on you making you spill your drink. When Jill rang to tell me that a couple of the kids from Shona's massive brood had been a bit poorly so the food was being brought in by a catering company because Shona hadn't had the time to do it herself the party seemed a little more attractive. I hoped she hadn't had time to make any of her strange wine either. Jill went on to tell me that apparently it was to be a bit of a glamorous event, some of the more famous of Jed's clients in the pop and rock world were rumoured to be attending and the kids were being minded by a babysitter for the night. There was the possibility that the party would turn out not to be so bad and, after all, I was doing bugger all else. I made a bit of an effort with a sparkly black dress that flattered my figure with the help of some large, firm support knickers underneath and a bit more makeup than usual. I even blow dried my hair carefully although I don't know I bothered as I knew it would tease me by looking great for ten minutes then laugh at my efforts and resume it's usual lank boring flatness before I'd even left the house. Oh well, it made me feel better knowing I'd at least tried. I just wouldn't look at it for the rest of the night and pretend to myself it looked as good as it did right after I'd finished styling it only to be shocked to see the state of it in pictures later.

I arrived at Shona's around eight to find the party in full swing. Shona, actually looking quite nice in a dress that wasn't one of her homemade efforts and without a swollen pregnant belly for a change, greeted me at the door "No Ben?" she questioned as she hugged me and then relieved me of my coat.

"No, he couldn't make it. Besides, it's not really that kind of relationship" I explained. I had asked Ben if he would like to come but he'd made some sort of vague excuse as to why he couldn't. Actually, thinking about it, I never did see him on a Saturday night. I had been a little disappointed when he'd said he couldn't make it, I had been hoping to introduce him to my friends at long last but, as I was increasingly having to remind myself, it was just a casual thing, he wasn't my partner, just a friend with benefits. As such I had no right to expect him to accompany me to things like this.

"Aww, that's a shame, I was hoping he'd be with you, I was really looking forward to meeting him. Let me get you a drink. Wine?"

Nettle, elderflower, dandelion, sprout? I wondered what delightful flavour she had to offer today. Better play it safe "Erm, not really in a wine mood, do you have Vodka?"

"Yep. With tonic?"

"Yes please"

Shona disappeared to hang up my coat and get me my drink and I took a look around at some of the guests. There were quite a lot of people there already including some quite good looking men who could potentially be single. Mmm things were looking up. I spied Jill talking to Becky and Paul and walked over to them. As I approached them I studied Paul, still amazed by Becky's revelation that he played away, with her blessing, and that he was a bit of a kinky bugger. My brain just couldn't make the connection between this quiet, bespectacled, slightly pudgy, affable man and kinky sex. I'd never look at him the same way again. He smiled as I approached and kissed me on the cheek "Hello, beautiful, how are you?" he said "Not seen you in a long time, where have you been hiding?"

"Ah just busy with work." I replied trying

my hardest not to think of him naked and being pissed on.

The party actually turned out to be pretty good. I mingled, saying hello to a few people that I knew and introducing myself to those I didn't. I spent a few minutes chatting to a drummer, a big muscular guy called Zak (suspect that wasn't his real name). Zak had bulging biceps and lots of impressive tattoos but a questionable IQ. He said "ya know" after every other sentence and seemed to think it was fine to squeeze my arse and stare without shame at my tits. He took me on a not very interesting journey of his many tattoos explaining, painstakingly and in great detail, the meaning behind each one and where he had gotten it. Then told me he was staying the night in a bed and breakfast down the road and invited me to go back with him for a nightcap, by which of course he meant a shag. I thought briefly of Ben, reminded myself we were in an open relationship and maybe did kind of half contemplate it for a little while. Then he introduced me to a wiry, pale, ginger bloke called Bobby with thick framed black glasses and blubbery lips who spat when he spoke. Bobby offered me a line of coke, which I politely declined and Zak asked if I'd ever fancied a threesome. Both men looked at me expectantly. No thanks. I made my excuses and buggered off sharpish to find Jill. I found her chatting to an extraordinarily beautiful, exotic looking, dark haired woman. They looked to be getting on very, very well indeed judging by their body language so rather than interrupt I went to see who else I could find.

I noticed a man standing on his own at the back of the room looking through Jed's extensive CD collection. I couldn't see his face as his head was bent down and he had his back towards me but something about his stance and his hair reminded me of someone. Walking over towards him he looked up at me and I was surprised and pleased to see it was Neil. "Oh, hi Red." He said and bent to kiss me on my cheek.

"Hello, fancy seeing you here." I said smiling at him.

"How do you know Jed and Shona?" He asked. I explained how Jill had met Shona at the anti-fracking demonstration and then introduced her to the rest of us. It turned out Neil knew Jed through working together years ago when he had been a sound engineer. They'd hit it off and been friends for about twelve years.

"Small world" we both said in unison and laughed.

"Let me get you a drink," offered Neil, indicating my empty glass.

I handed it over to him "Thanks, Vodka and tonic please."

"OK. Guard that spot, I'll be right back" A few minutes later he was back with two full glasses. He handed me mine and we clinked them together. "To friends," he said.

"I'll drink to that. Cheers!"

We chatted for a while whilst we sipped our drinks. Once our glasses were empty he asked me if I wanted to go back to his for a while. "I assure you I have only gentlemanly intentions." he said, taking my hand and kissing the back of it "Purely platonic if you want it to be I promise. I just enjoy your company and this party is beginning to get a bit boring."

"I enjoy your company too." I said smiling but, even though it was me that had set the boundaries of the relationship, I was feeling a little disappointed about it being platonic and wondering if I could trust myself if I went home with him. "Go on then, phone a taxi. But only if you've got some of that excellent whiskey left for a nightcap."

"I most certainly have." he said with a wink.

"In that case, let's get out of here." We said our goodbyes and left to a few raised eyebrows. Noticing the raised eyebrows Neil put his arm around my shoulders and said loudly "Come on sexy, can't wait to get you into bed." Laughing, I elbowed him in the ribs.

Back at Neil's place we had a great couple of hours chatting, playing cards for pennies and drinking far too much whiskey. I was thoroughly enjoying myself but as the time crept towards 3am I found I was having difficulty keeping my eyes open. "I think I need a taxi" I said reluctantly.

"Stay here" said Neil, "I have a very big, very comfortable bed and even though you are one sexy lady I promise I will leave your virtue intact. I'll even sleep on the couch if you'd prefer?"

"Don't be daft, it's your bed. I trust you. It's myself I don't trust!" I did find him very attractive, and I loved his company but it just wouldn't be fair on Neil to take things any further when I wasn't willing to let go of Ben. We went upstairs where he found me a spare toothbrush and a pyjama top to sleep in. "Platonic cuddling is allowed if it's OK with you" I said when he came out of the bathroom and climbed into bed next to me. He was looking very sexy and manly wearing just a pair of checked pyjama bottoms that matched the top I was wearing. A neat line of hair rose enticingly out of the waistband ending just below his belly button, I wanted to kiss it. I have a thing about men's belly's, also love dimples and strong upper arms. I'm a bit strange I know, I don't deny it.

"Absolutely." He replied "In fact I insist on it, considering you have stolen my top you will need to keep me warm. And, I happen to be a world class cuddler. I have won prizes for it." I snuggled up to him happily and gave him a sleepy kiss on the cheek loving the prickly feel of his beard on my lips. He smelt of soap and toothpaste. As promised his bed was comfy and warm and we soon fell asleep. No funny business, although it was hard to resist pouncing on him and

I think if I hadn't been so tired I might have done so.

CHAPTER TWELVE

The next morning I was woken by the sun shining through the window onto my face. I wondered briefly where I was before it came back to me, turning over sleepily I found Neil's side of the bed empty but still warm. Smiling to myself I stretched and yawned then got up and made my way to the bathroom. Out on the landing I could hear Neil downstairs singing along somewhat out of tune to the radio "don't give up the day job!" I shouted down.

"Ah, good morning lazy bones." he replied popping his head out of the kitchen and looking up the stairs at me "Coffee? Bacon roll? How's the head?"

"Yes please and actually it's not that bad considering the amount of whiskey you made me drink!"

I did what I needed to do in the bathroom then made my way down to the kitchen, the delicious smell of bacon and coffee making my stomach growl in anticipation. As we sat and ate breakfast listening to the radio happy and content in each other's company I reflected on how natural it all felt with Neil, it was like I'd known him for years. We seemed to fit easily together, had just clicked straight away, he'd make a great boyfriend, He was great looking, funny, kind, just a shame I was so hooked up on Ben.

A couple of days later, Ben and I went out for an Italian. "How was the party the other night?" He asked "Meet anyone famous? Get off with anyone?"

"It was good, shame you couldn't come. There were a couple of seen better days rock stars, and I chatted to a drummer for a while." I told him

"No sex?"

"Nope. Although I did get the offer of a threesome with the drummer and his friend, which I turned down." I didn't feel the need to share the fact that I had spent the night with Neil and besides we hadn't done anything.

"That's a shame, I would have enjoyed listening to you tell me about it." Said Ben with a grin. "You know, I've been thinking" He said, taking my hand and looking at me earnestly "How would you feel about being exclusive? Just dating each other? I don't think I want to share my beautiful creature with anyone else anymore."

I was shocked, and confused. In one breath he's telling me he would like to hear about me having sex with another man and in the next he's asking me to date him exclusively. Really? Having an exclusive relationship with Ben was something I'd tried not to think about because I didn't think that it would be something he would be interested in but truthfully it was what I'd wanted. I had found myself falling for him and I was no longer happy with the idea of sharing him with other people either. Had never really been happy with that idea to be honest. I'd even been thinking about stopping seeing him because I wasn't enjoying our arrangement any more, I just wasn't cut out for sharing a man I had feelings for no matter how modern and understanding I tried to be. I thought about it for a moment, I really liked Neil but my insane addiction to Ben won. "I think I would like that," I admitted, smiling at him.

"I have a confession." He said "I saw Ellen on Saturday night" his other friend with benefits. I knew he had been with someone else all those Saturday nights "I told her about my feelings for you. She didn't take it very well and we decided to stop seeing each other. That's when I realised, you're all I need. You're all I want. I know I said we needed to guard our feelings because of my personal situation and it will be difficult to have a full on relationship but the truth is, I am falling in love with you."

I stared at him speechless, that was the last thing I was expecting him to say to me. I was a little puzzled too, I mean what exactly was his personal situation? Of course I knew he lived with Gina but they weren't together, he'd told me she was practically just his lodger. So why couldn't he have a proper, full on relationship with someone? Was he lying to me?

"It's all your fault" he continued "You're just so warm and loving. The way you look at me and the way you hold me, I had no chance."

I'd had no agenda. I was just being me, I found it difficult to be cold, I could separate sex from love easily enough but I was still quite a tactile person who cared about other people and enjoyed the closeness of the act as much as the sex itself. Yes, I enjoyed a good seeing to, but deep down I was a hugs and kisses kind of girl. And he wasn't entirely blameless, he hugged and kissed me too and rang me all the time and told me I was beautiful. "I think I'm falling in love with you too. But I'm scared to death." I admitted. I was scared, the last thing I wanted was to fall in love, it never worked out for me, I always ended up with a broken heart. When I loved, I loved hard and my poor heart was battered and full of scars from past relationships.

"I won't hurt you. I know how hurt you've been in the past. I'll look after your heart, it'll be safe with me." he promised. The liar.

CHAPTER THIRTEEN

The following weekend it was the girl's Christmas do. Danny, my ex, used to scoff at me calling my group of friends "The Girls", said we were too old to be referring to ourselves as girls but he could fuck off, we would always be the girls even when we're old and grey and causing havoc together in some nursing home somewhere. He was only jealous because no one liked him and he had no friends. For the last fifteen years or so the girls all met up one Saturday in December at the Hare and Hounds, had a cheap turkey dinner and a few drinks before going on to a club. The food wasn't the greatest but it was edible and more importantly the drinks were cheap. The landlord was very accommodating of a large group of raucous women, probably because we spent a fortune on booze and we always had a really good time. This year there were twelve of us tarted up to the nines and all dressed to impress looking gorgeous in lovely, mostly black, sparkly outfits. I was sitting next to Becky and we were chatting away when I received a picture message. It was from Ben, a photograph of Gina in a hospital bed. Although she was looking rather poorly she was laughing and holding a cardboard sick bowl on her head.

"Who's that?" asked Becky looking at my phone.

"It's Ben's err" what was she exactly? I settled on lodger "I told you about her before, she's really poorly."

"Ah right. His lodger." She was staring at the picture with a strange expression "Is that an engagement ring she's wearing?"

Whaaat?! I peered at the picture. "Zoom in on her hand." urged Becky. I zoomed in and we both studied Gina's hand for a moment. "Looks like an engagement ring to me" she said. It looked like an engagement ring to me too.

"Could it be like, you know, that mirror effect you sometimes get when you take a picture?" I suggested

"So it looks like her left hand but really it could be her right?"

"Possibly" We looked some more. "No, I do think it is her left. And it looks a bit too flashy to be just a normal ring" said Becky

"Maybe there's a rational explanation, maybe she has a fiancé that's not Ben." I said even though I didn't believe it.

"Maybe, but then why does she live with Ben

and not him?" Said Becky. She had a point.

The picture kind of put a downer on the whole night. The elated feeling I'd had since Ben had told me he was falling in love with me popped like a balloon. I tried my hardest not to think about it and have a good time but I had a big knot of tension in my stomach the whole night that no amount of drink and lovely company could unravel. I wanted to text or phone Ben straight away and demand an explanation but decided to wait until I next saw him. It was harder to lie to someone face to face.

It was Wednesday before I next saw Ben and I'd managed to wind myself up into a right old state about Gina and the bloody ring. Despite him telling me he was falling in love with me I still had huge doubts about him and seeing the ring had intensified them. My gut instinct was telling me not to trust him and I am usually a great believer in trusting your instincts so why was I not taking heed this time? He arrived at my house right on time as usual, smiling and holding a bunch of pale orange roses. "They're only from the garage," he said, handing them over to me "but I saw them and they reminded me of you, beautiful and unusual." A week ago I'd have been thrilled with the flowers and the compliment but today I just thought more cheap, corny bullshit.

"Thanks, I'll just pop them in some water." I said taking the flowers into the kitchen and shoving them into a vase not even bothering to take them out of the plastic wrapper. I brought them back into the living room and placed them on the table. Ben came over and hugged me tightly. I let him hold me for a moment breathing in his lovely smell then I stepped back from him.

"We need to talk" I said

"Oh? Sounds ominous" he said, sitting on the sofa and looking at me expectantly.

I sat in the chair opposite him and took a deep breath, I hate confrontation and was really hoping this wouldn't develop into an argument but it had to be asked "What's the deal with you and Gina? The truth Ben. Are you being totally honest with me about your relationship with her?"

"Of course I am, why would I lie to you?"

Why indeed? "Well, it's just that I couldn't help but notice that she was wearing an engagement ring in that photo you sent me the other day, so what's the score there?"

He looked angry, always a sure sign of guilt. "Yes, I bought her a ring, but it was years ago and it doesn't mean anything any more. The woman is dying for God's sake, what do you want me to do? Take the fucking ring off her?" he said, his voice loud.

She was just his lodger but she was wearing his engagement ring? Something wasn't adding up quite right here. "Truthfully, it just all seems a bit odd to me." I said

"What are you saying? You don't believe me?"

"I honestly don't know what to believe," I said

"you never stay overnight with me, you live with her and now I discover she's wearing your engagement ring. Like I said, it's all a bit weird."

"I told you about Gina and our living arrangement before I even met you. Don't you trust me?"

"I want to trust you, but.." I shrugged, I didn't know what else to say. The truth of the matter was no, I didn't trust him. Him telling me about the arrangement with Gina could have been a double bluff for all I knew.

He got to his feet angrily "Right, well, I'm off then. Ring me if you decide you can trust me otherwise there really isn't any point in continuing with this is there?"

He left slamming the door behind him. That went well I thought miserably, staring at the orange roses and trying not to cry.

CHAPTER FOURTEEN

Christmas came and went with the usual too much food, too much drink, visiting family members you hadn't seen for ages and in all honesty didn't really like all that much. Generally trying to make merry and share good-will as the season demanded but not quite get-ting there. Of course falling out with Ben had also put a damper on things and turned me into a big-ger Scrooge than usual.

It was a few days later when I heard from him. I had considered messaging him a couple of times but thought better of it. I'd been falling for him, I was miserable and missed him but per-haps it was for the best that it was over. The sex had been fantastic, out of this world, but the rest of it had been weird and had caused me a lot of anxiety and doubt. You couldn't have a relation-ship based just on sex, well you couldn't if you had feelings for that person anyway. I considered calling Neil but decided against it for now. I had to give myself a little time and space to get over Ben, make sure it was truly over. I didn't want to base a new relationship on a rebound, that wouldn't be fair on anyone.

Sunday afternoon as I sat watching an old disaster movie with a bowl of popcorn, my guilty pleasures, my phone pinged. Message from Ben -

I'm so sorry Scarlett, I know
how things must look. Can we
talk? I miss you so much xx

No, I don't think that's
a good idea. Sorry.

I know what you're thinking
and yes you're right I haven't
been totally honest with you
but it's not what it seems.
I owe you an explanation xx

I'm not interested.
Please leave me alone.

I can't. I've never felt
like this about anyone before
and I didn't think I ever would
after getting to my age. I can't
just let you go. I love you so much xx

Did he love me? I wasn't sure I believed him. Should I give him another chance? I had missed him, or at least I thought I had but did I love him or was I just missing the sex? I was so confused about everything.

Please babe just give me
the chance to explain
everything to you then if

you want me to go then I'll go xx

OK, but I want the truth

Of course.
Please can I have some xxx's ?

No.

Against my better judgement I agreed to see him a couple of days later. I just couldn't help myself, I missed him too much. I was addicted to him. He wanted to see me straight away but I said no, I lied and said I was busy, I needed to give myself an illusion of control over the relationship which I knew in reality I didn't have.

The next day, Monday I got up unusually early for me. I hadn't slept well and in the end decided to get up and get on with some of the chores I'd been neglecting. I wasn't the world's tidiest person and my house, as small as it was, soon ended up looking a right state If I didn't keep on top of it. I finished cleaning the house by lunchtime and was at a loss at what to do with myself for the rest of the day. I even considered doing some ironing for a moment but told myself not to be silly. I didn't even know if my iron worked, it was that long since it had seen the light of day. Most of my clothes were made out of fabrics that didn't crease, a major consideration when I purchased anything.

It was that funny period of time that falls between Christmas and New Year, the festive twilight zone. There was nothing worth watching on the telly, you felt fat and lazy and shit because you'd eaten too much crap and drank too much alcohol, the Christmas decorations were still up but you were sick of the sight of them and you longed for normality. I made myself a lunch of cheese, crackers and pickled onions and ate it at the kitchen table staring out into the back garden. It was cold, grey and wet outside, already starting to go a little dark and I decided I would enjoy a nice quiet, relaxing afternoon curled up with Walter, a nice cup of tea and a good book. I was actually sick of the sight of booze by this point so the wine was staying where it was, chilling in the fridge. My fake log burner was on as were my fairy lights and I lit a couple of candles. It was all warm and cosy. I settled on the sofa with some chocolate and opened a new book that Jill had given me as a Christmas gift, one that I'd been after reading for a long time. I had a Kindle but there was something special about a brand new book with its crisp pages and that new book smell that you just didn't get with an eBook. I had read the first couple of chapters and was just escaping into the story when my phone rang. I should have turned the bloody thing off I thought as I reached for it annoyed at being interrupted. I looked at the screen, it was Ben. "Hello" I said, a little tetchy. I was still pissed off with him.

"Hiya beautiful, what are you up to today? I really want to see you, let's sort things out." said

Ben

My brain said no, but somewhere between there and my mouth it changed to a yes. I needed to see him to sort everything out between us and to be honest, I was horny.

"Great! I have a bit of a problem though, I can't really come over to you, Gina is still in hospital and I can't leave the dog. Would you like to come over here?"

He wanted me to go to his house, the one he shared with Gina? "I do want to see you, but don't think I'd be comfortable coming to your house" I said.

"It's OK, really it is. I've spoken to Gina and she's totally fine with it. Come over, you can stay the night if you want. It's not like you'll be sleeping in her bed, we've got separate rooms."

Spend a whole night with him? Well that would be a novelty, It was also quite presumptuous of him to think I would want to stay, he still had some explaining to do about the engagement ring.

"Please babe, I'm missing you. I'll take you for a nice meal" he said, picking up on my reluctance when I didn't answer him and trying to bribe me with my other weakness, food.

I contemplated it for a moment, the promise of a nice meal swaying me. Food always won, I love good food and good sex and if I went over I would be probably be treated to both "OK, but only if you're a hundred percent sure it's alright with Gina and that we can go for curry. And don't forget, before we do anything you still owe me an explanation about the ring."

"I know, I promise I will tell you everything and of course it's OK, it is my house after all. Curry it is"

He gave me his address. I got showered and changed, packed my overnight bag, fed Walter and drove over to Ben's house for the first time. I arrived around six, not sure what to expect. Ben opened the door and welcomed me in with a kiss. Showing me into the living room he introduced me to his dog, an overexcited Springer Spaniel named Max. Max was a real cutie who, like most pupsters, was just absolutely over the moon to meet me going by the enthusiastic tail wagging and frenzied licking of my hand. He was so excited that he peed a little on my shoe but that was OK, sometimes I peed a little too when I didn't mean to so I completely understood. Ben, embarrassed, apologised for the pee on behalf of the dog. I told him not to worry, it was only a shoe and an old one at that but he worried and fussed, insisting on cleaning it for me with a kitchen wipe. He managed to calm Max down then invited me to sit down for a moment whilst he went to finish getting ready.

I looked around, the house was very modern and mostly grey therefore not really to my taste as I preferred something more traditional with a bit more character and colour but still it was nice. It was very nicely decorated, clean, tidy and definitely spoke of a feminine presence with the ornaments, pictures and soft furnishings that had been chosen. I perched on the edge of the grey sofa feeling a little out of place and uncomfortable whilst Ben went to feed the dog and get his coat. The tasteful pink and gold Christmas decorations were still up and I noticed there were several cards on the wall. There were a couple of cards of the type - To a Special Couple, and To the Both of You but two in particular stood out. To the One I Love and To my Fiancé. For fucks sake, what?! I stood up and walked over so I could read inside. To Gina, my best friend, I love you, Ben x and To my Ben bear, thank you for always being there for me. Can't wait to marry you. Merry Christmas, with love always and forever Gina xxx "Right then, enough of this shit and lies!" I muttered to myself, I was fuming. Without a word to Ben I picked up my bag and left, slamming the door behind me hard enough to make the windows rattle then drove my car home like I'd stolen it. My phone rang nonstop all the way but I didn't trust myself to talk to him, especially whilst I was driving I was fucking livid and I probably would have crashed my car. I had several messages when I finally arrived home, both voicemail and text. He was totally confused as to why I'd left. Once I'd calmed down a little I finally answered him. "The cards mate, that's why I left. You're such a liar."

"Cards, what cards? What are you talking about" he sounded genuinely perplexed

"The fucking Christmas cards. You know "To my Fiancé, To the one I love", those cards."

He inhaled sharply and muttered "shit" under his breath "Ah, oh, right. Look, er, I can explain."

"Oh really? Again? Well this should be interesting, go ahead. This better be good. I'm sick to death of this bullshit."

"Look Scarlett, you're very angry right now, and I get it. I totally understand why you would be but I promise you things are not quite what they seem."

I had heard this before, but how on earth was he going to weasel his way out of this one this time? "And just how much more quite what they seem, can Gina writing in a card that she can't wait to marry you be? Seems pretty straightforward to me. Is she your fiancée or not?" I asked.

"Look, we need to talk, but face to face. Please come back, or I can come over to you for an hour or so."

I didn't know what to do. My head was telling me to tell him to fuck off but my heart was saying listen to what he has to say. I was also curious to hear how he would spin this one.

"I'll think about it, but I don't want to see you tonight, I'm far too angry. I'll ring you tomorrow. If I decide I want to see you." I told him.

"OK" he said in a winey sad little voice that made me even madder "I do love you, you know."

"Yeah, whatever" I said scornfully and ended the call without a goodbye. This was when you missed having a phone with a handset you could slam down. Stabbing the call end button on a mobile just didn't give you the same satisfaction. And I broke my bloody nail on my phone screen whilst doing it which made me even madder still.

I didn't call him the next day. He called me several times and sent me a load of messages but I ignored all contact from him. Let him sweat, I thought, but it felt like it was me who was being punished.

CHAPTER FIFTEEN

I managed two days before I finally gave in and spoke to Ben. I was still livid with him and very confused about what the hell was going on but I missed him so much. There was a constant knot of anxiety in my stomach, I could hardly eat anything (which definitely wasn't like me. As you've probably gathered I am very much a live to eat kind of girl) I couldn't sleep properly, I couldn't concentrate on work. Everytime my phone rang or pinged with a message my stomach lurched hoping it would be him. I just didn't know what to do with myself and I needed to sort this out one way or another. He sounded very relieved when I called him "I'm missing you so much babe" he said.

"I'm missing you too" I admitted "but I'm so confused about everything and so bloody angry with you."

"Gina is home from the hospital now, can I come over tonight to see you, to explain."

"Is she better?" I asked, not that I really cared to be honest (yes, I can be a bitch) but it seemed like the polite thing to say.

"A lot better than she was." He replied

"Good. OK, come over later but just to talk, nothing else. I want to know what the hell is going on."

He turned up just before eight. He tried to hug me when I opened the door but I turned and walked away from him. He shrugged and followed me inside. Seeing him made me unsettled, nervous, and, although I hated myself for it, horny. My stomach was in knots but I was feeling aroused. My brain didn't have a bloody clue what was going on with all the mixed signals my body was sending it. I told Ben to sit on the settee whilst I made us a cup of tea using the excuse to go into the kitchen to try to compose myself a little. I brought the tea in, put it on the table then sat in the chair opposite him. "OK, go ahead," I said sitting back and crossing my arms "this better be good."

"Promise me you'll let me tell you the whole story. You can ask me questions or even throw things at me afterwards if you like but let me finish telling you first please."

"OK, I can do that." I said

"First of all, I'm sorry for misleading you. I do love you, that wasn't planned but it happened and it's the truth. Most of what I told you is the truth, how me and Gina met, me going to London, me wanting to end the relationship, her getting poorly," he took a deep breath, "but.. well, truthfully she is more than my lodger. We are still in a relationship."

Even though I had known this, it had been obvious from the cards, my temper still flared, I jumped to my feet " I fucking knew it!" I shouted at him angrily.

"Please, Scarlett, sit down, let me finish, you promised."

I had promised so fuming, I sat down. Arms and legs crossed, foot bouncing, glaring at him with my best evil look of contempt. So what was the deal here? Was he going to tell me that he was going to leave her for me? Could I even let him do that to a woman who was dying and who obviously loved him? Did I even want to continue with this relationship after all these lies?

"We, that's Gina and I, well we're in a polyamorous relationship. That is we are not monogamous. What I mean is well, it's not just an open relationship where we have sex with other people just for the fun of it, although that's been part of it too with the swinging, but we don't limit ourselves to just one relationship. We have romantic relationships with other people. We practice ethical non-monogamy where we are open and honest with each other and we believe that you can have feelings for more than one person at a time. She honestly knows about me and you. I've told her how I feel about you and we have her full blessing."

"Shame you weren't open and honest with me then. Why did you lie to me? Why let me believe you are not in a relationship?" I asked.

He looked away a little shamefaced. " I don't know, I'm sorry. When you and I first met it was just supposed to be a bit of fun and great sex, I didn't know I was going to fall in love with you, I had no intention of that happening, but then once I realised I was falling in love with you it was too late. I was scared of telling you in case I lost you. Most people just don't get polyamory."

"So didn't you think I would ever find out? What was your plan? You were hoping perhaps Gina would die before I found out and I'd never need to know? Where is my choice in all of this? I should have been aware that I was getting myself into this polyamorous relationship so it could have been my decision whether I wanted to or not. You deliberately deceived me."

"I know. For what it's worth I am very sorry"

You're only sorry because you've been found out, I thought to myself. "So, do you sleep together, are you getting married? You asked me to go exclusive with you, are we exclusive, obviously other than your fiancée or are you still pursuing other relationships?" I had a hundred questions I wanted to ask.

"Gina and I do sleep in the same bed, but we've not had sex in a long time. We do have plans to get married in the summer. If she lives that long that is. Not that I really want to get married to be honest, marriage was never in the plan with me and her but it's one of her dying wishes to have a nice wedding and when she dies things like our finances and her life insurance will be simpler to sort out if she's my wife"

"How romantic" I muttered. I was furious with him and couldn't believe what I was hearing.

He stood up and came over to my chair crouching beside me. He took hold of my hand and looked at me. "I promise you what I said about loving you and being exclusive is true, I am not looking for anyone else. I really hope we can work this out," he said.

I pulled my hand away. "I think you'd better leave and let me process all this." I said reluctantly. I was missing the sex but I couldn't let his seduction of me in the bedroom influence my decision about our relationship "I need some time."

"OK" he said sadly standing up. He picked up his jacket "I don't want to go but I totally understand. I'll call you tomorrow, if that's OK?" He bent down and kissed me on my cheek then left. I looked at the mugs of tea on the table, untouched, going cold. My mind was in turmoil, what was I going to do?

CHAPTER SIXTEEN

The next day was New Years Eve and I was supposed to be going to a party with Jess. I had hardly slept, everything was just going around and around in my mind. Then, when I did eventually fall asleep, I had troubled dreams and woke up in a foul mood feeling more tired than I was when I went to bed. The last thing I felt like doing was going to a party but I couldn't let her down at the last minute. I hadn't yet spoken to any of my friends about what had been going on with Ben over Christmas, I was still trying to get my head around it all. I was furious about him deceiving me but didn't want to lose what we had. I felt like I loved him, but maybe it was just that I was in lust with him? I just couldn't figure it out but one thing I did know for certain was that I didn't want to lose him.

I dragged myself out of bed and went down to the kitchen where I brewed a carafe of coffee and fed Walter something that smelt disgusting which he devoured noisily and with great enthusiasm. "Rude" I said to him, referring to his lack of table manners. He didn't care. I then sat on the settee deep in thought sipping the strong hot brew. My phone rang, Jill.

"Gooood morning!" She trilled cheerfully, she is always Little Miss Prozac in the mornings, me, not so much.

"Hiya" I replied, a little sullenly

"Well, someone sounds full of the joys this morning. Hungover?" She asked

"No, not at all, just a bit fed up. Ben came up and explained a few things last night and I'm not quite sure what to think about what he's told me."

"Oh? Good things or bad things, actually, don't answer that, obviously bad things judging by your mood."

"Not exactly bad things but not good things either. Just the truth and I don't know how to deal with it."

"The truth? I'm guessing you mean about him and Gina the lodger? Go on.."

"I can't really explain over the phone, it's a bit complicated. Do you fancy meeting for breakfast at the cafe? I could do with getting out of the house for a bit. Getting a bit of fresh air."

"OK, see you at Penny's in half an hour. And this better be good because I've already had breakfast and you'll be making me have another one!"

I arrived at Penny's, it was really quiet. Apart from Francis the wheelchair bound old man who was there so much he was almost part of the furniture and the staff which consisted of Penny and her daughter Sarah, we had the place to ourselves. We ordered coffees and bacon sandwiches and then sat down, as far away from Francis as we could. He was a lovely man but he usually smelt of stale piss and could talk the hind leg off a donkey, I know he was probably just lonely but I really wasn't in the mood for him that morning. I began to explain to Jill what Ben had told me the night before.

"Well" she said after I finished "I'm not quite sure what to say. What are you going to do? Are you going to keep on seeing him?"

"I don't know, I think so, but I'm not sure. I'm still not 100% sure he's telling me the whole truth. It's all so bloody weird."

"Well, why don't you call his bluff? Tell him you want to meet Gina and ask her about their relationship."

That, I thought, was an excellent idea. I ate my bacon butty and ordered a Danish pastry. "Careful fatty, you don't want to be putting all that weight back on that you've lost." commented Jill. I'd been a right porker after my long term relationship with my ex Danny had ended but had managed to shift a few stone over the last year or so by kicking my fast food and ice cream habits and eating healthily most of the time. I was no longer obese but I was, and probably always would be a little on the plump side. Or curvy as I preferred to call myself.

"It's still Christmas, doesn't count. Back to healthy eating tomorrow. My new year resolution is to get fit and slim." I said biting into the treat, bits of flaky pastry going everywhere.

"Don't forget, easier on than off." She was right there. I put weight on just thinking about unhealthy food but it took a whole week of willpower to shift a pound or two. "I'm thinking of giving up drinking for New Year." She announced without warning.

"What? Alcohol?" I asked, shocked.

"Well yes. I mean I'd still need to drink water and stuff or I'd get terribly dehydrated. And coffee, I couldn't give up coffee"

"But why?" I cried. This was a disaster, Jill was my drinking buddy, who would I get drunk with if she decided to go teetotal?

"Because I drink too much" which meant by association she thought I drank too much too "I'm too old to keep making a dick of myself and it's just not doing me any favours health wise."

Again, she had a point but I liked having a drink or four occasionally. It took the nasty sharp edges off life and made things pleasantly fuzzy and more bearable. I had a drink when I was pissed off, when I was bored, when I was sad. I realised I was using it as a crutch and I'd been steadily drinking more since I'd met Ben.

I'd hardly drank alone before meeting him but lately I had been downing a bottle of wine or a couple of whiskeys most evenings. If I wasn't careful it could turn into a problem, and it was an expensive habit. "I don't think I could give up entirely, but it wouldn't do any harm to cut down a little I suppose." I said.

"Let's put the money we save from booze into a holiday fund." suggested Jill, "You say you're always too skint to go away but I bet you could easily save twenty quid a week if you didn't drink so much. That would easily pay for a holiday. It would give you some motivation too." She was right, it was a good idea, and a holiday would give me something to look forward to.

Later that afternoon Ben rang me. "Hiya babe, have you had a chance to think about what I told you. Do you need more time?"

"I've thought about it." I replied "I'm still not sure what to make of it all to be honest. And frankly, I'm still bloody furious at you for lying to me."

"I am really, really, sorry. I promise, no more lies and I will make it up to you."

"OK. But before I make my mind up, I'd like to meet Gina."

He was quiet for a moment. "Do you still not trust me?" He asked a little petulantly.

"Would you, in my position?"

There were a few more moments of silence as he

considered this "No, I guess not, OK, I'll ask her." he said a little reluctantly

And that's how I found myself, a few days later on a freezing cold, grey January day, nervously driving to Ben's house to meet his fiancée. Apparently Gina was more than happy to meet me. I marvelled at this whilst I was driving. "I'm going to meet my boyfriend's fiancée" I said to my reflection in the rear view mirror "what the actual fuck is going on?" My reflection declined to comment on this madness.

I arrived at his house with no idea what to expect. Ben opened the door, looking a little nervous himself but with a big smile. He let me inside, kissing me on the cheek, taking my jacket and hanging it up in the little hallway. Max came out to greet me wagging his tail excitedly and I took a moment to pet and fuss over him trying to settle my nerves before Ben shooed him away worrying he might pee on my shoes again. My stomach felt like it was doing somersaults, almost like I was going into a very important job interview. At least I had experience of job interviews, I'd had no experience of meeting my lover's other half before. I hadn't been able to find any tips on the internet about dealing with this unprecedented situation, only tips on meeting the parents or friends. Perhaps there was an opportunity to set up a support group?

I had taken ages and great care to choose

my clothes and do my makeup, worrying about looking too tarty but wanting to look nice. I'd settled on my best jeans and a nice green top that wasn't too revealing but wasn't too mumsy either. Both were charity shop finds that I'd been rather chuffed with.

To be honest the whole thing was a little underwhelming. Gina was absolutely lovely. She welcomed me warmly into their home with a hug and offered me a cup of tea saying she was very pleased to meet me at last. There were so many questions I wanted to ask her, that I maybe should have asked her in retrospect but they felt inappropriate and invasive so we ended up just having a general chit chat about everyday things. Ben looked as nervous as I felt but all in all everything went well. I left after about half an hour. Looking relieved that the meeting was over Ben walked me to my car and gave me a quick kiss on the cheek. "OK?" He asked

"OK" I said "She really is lovely."

"She is" he agreed "Can I see you tomorrow?"

"Yes, OK, tomorrow." And there we were, back on again.

CHAPTER SEVENTEEN

January dragged on and on. There was no snow but it was cold and wet and miserable. Work was boring me to tears and things were still a little strained between me and Ben. Half of me wanted to end the relationship, it was still causing me a lot of stress, and the other half of me couldn't let him go. When I was with him the rest of the world disappeared and I was totally content and happy and not to mention sexually satisfied. When I wasn't with him I wondered where he was and who he was with and convinced myself he was lying to me.

I received another strange gift from my mystery stalker, a box of sex toys including a remote controlled vibrating butt plug that Jill found highly amusing. I kept the police informed of the new gift. I was a little hesitant to tell them about it at first, it was embarrassing, but, as Jill reasoned, they were probably used to much weirder stuff than unwanted sex toy deliveries. “You should try it out, it intensifies your orgasm, feels amazing.” she informed me knowledgeably, taking the butt plug out of the box and switching it on. It was only small but it was very powerful. I decided to take her word for it, I didn’t really fancy it. Besides what if I had to turn it in for evidence and it had been up my arse?

We crawled towards the end of the month and my birthday which fell on a Friday that year. An excellent day for a birthday in my opinion because it meant you could stretch the celebrations out for the whole weekend. Waking up in my big bed all by myself that morning I felt a brief moment of loneliness. I was feeling a little sorry for myself knowing that Ben would be waking up with Gina and I found myself, not for the first time, wishing I was in a normal relationship not one where I had to share my man with somebody else. Still, Ben had promised to take me away to stay in a nice hotel on Saturday, and actually stay overnight with me for the first time so I was excited about that and looking forward to it very much indeed.

I yawned and stretched, accidentally kicking Walter off the end of the bed where he had been curled up asleep by my feet. “Whoops! Sorry mate.” I said apologising to him. He gave me a grumpy little miaow of contempt and then skulked out of the door eyeballing me with his very best feline glare of pure evilness. Getting out of bed I opened the curtains to find blue skies and a little bit of sunshine which helped to lift my spirits. Turning on the radio I hummed along to the music whilst I showered and got dressed. Usually I slobbed around in my pyjamas until nearly lunchtime (one of the perks of working from home) but I had plans that morning to meet Jill and Becky for an early birthday breakfast at Penny's cafe.

I had a lovely breakfast with the girls. Jill gave me a navy blue dressing gown with silver stars made out of the softest fabric I had ever felt and instructed me to burn my tatty old grey one as soon as I got home. Becky gave me a gift voucher for the hair salon she went to, promising me that they could do wonders with my stupid, unruly hair. " It is our intention this year to stop you looking like a mental patient!" laughed Jill. Charming!

Penny, the owner of the cafe, presented me with a large cupcake complete with a birthday candle after I finished my bacon and cheese toastie. Healthy eating had been suspended for my birthday. Laughing, the girls sang "Happy Birthday" to me slightly out of tune, totally embarrassing me.

"Make a wish" said Becky as I went to blow out my candle. What to wish for? Ben to be just mine? To stop being in love with him and find someone who could be just mine? I settled on happiness. I just wanted to be happy was that too much to ask for? I blew out the candle and ate the cake (which was delicious) with another cup of coffee. After Jill and Becky left for work I strolled home on a caffeine and sugar high, in the sunshine that had been a rare thing that winter. It was still cold but it was one of those lovely crisp winter days with clear blue skies. Wrapped up in my warm coat, hat and gloves I breathed in the clean cold air and marvelled to myself about the fact that I was now nearer fifty than forty. Where had the years gone and when would my mind cop on to the fact that I was middle aged? I still felt twenty five! I enjoyed the walk, my muscles, stretching and warming, the exercise releasing endorphins and making me feel good. I need to do this more often I thought to myself, I should get up in the morning and go for a walk before I start work instead of dossing about in my pyjamas most of the day. But I wouldn't, I was too bloody lazy. I arrived home, waving at Nosy Nancy from across the road who was peeping through her net curtains as usual. That woman should work for the CIA never mind neighbourhood watch, nothing escaped her notice. As I got to my front door deep in concentration trying to find the right key to open it a deep voice right behind me said "Scarlett!" Almost jumping out of my skin I turned around to find my next door but one neighbour Craig stood there in his pyjama bottoms and bare feet holding a white cake box. He must have been freezing.

"This came for you." He said holding out the

box.

"Oh, thanks." I said, taking it from him, it was quite heavy. Noticing my hands were shaking he asked me if I was OK. "Yes" I assured him with an embarrassed little laugh "Just didn't hear you, startled me a little!"

"Sorry, didn't mean to make you jump. See you later." Smiling at me and giving me a little salute he padded up the path and back to his own house.

I took the box into the house and placed it on the kitchen counter. Opening it I found a pink, heart shaped cake with happy birthday sexy bitch iced across the top. Another gift from my anonymous stalker. I wondered if they'd delivered it in person? Probably not but wouldn't hurt to ask. I walked around to Craig's and knocked on the door. "Hello again" I said when he answered "sorry to bother you but I was wondering who delivered the cake?"

"No problem, it was delivered in a little white van, a bakery I think but not Penny's. Might have been Turner's." he told me, his hand down the front of his pyjamas absentmindedly scratching his crotch. Nice. I thanked him and went home. Googling the number for Turners Bakery I gave them a call and enquired about the cake.

"Oh yes" said the pleasant lady who answered the phone "A lady ordered it on Monday to be delivered to you today. I thought it was a bit rude to put the word bitch on it to be honest but she was insistent, said it was her boss who wanted it, that you were his wife and that's what he called you for a joke." It amused me slightly that she almost whispered the word "bitch" as if saying it out loud wasn't allowed.

A woman? That was strange. Maybe she was my stalker's personal assistant "Not my husband, no. I'm not married. Did you happen to get a name at all?" I asked hopefully.

"Oh, right. No, sorry I didn't."

"Did she pay by card?"

"I don't think so. No, I think she paid cash."

"Can you remember what she looked like?" I asked hopefully

"Sorry, no, not really. We get a lot of customers. All I can remember is that I think she was average height, brown hair maybe. Is there a problem?" she sounded a little concerned and worried.

"No, it's OK." I assured her "Just someone playing pranks on me and I'm trying to get to the bottom of it that's all." I thanked her for her help and ended the call.

I took a photo of the cake using my phone and emailed it to PC Jenny Smith with a short explanation and details of the conversation with the lady from the bakery. I was still totally mystified as to who my mystery stalker was but it was obviously someone who knew my birthday as well as my favourite wine and chocolates.

CHAPTER EIGHTEEN

Later that night I met Jill and Becky at the pub for a few birthday drinks. I had debated throwing the cake in the bin but in the end I took it with me, after scraping off the writing, and gave it to Dominic behind the bar telling him to cut it up and give it to whoever wanted some. I certainly didn't want it but it seemed such a waste just to throw it away. After getting drinks we settled around a table debating who my mystery stalker could possibly be. Since I'd had my locks changed I hadn't had any more feelings of being watched or evidence that anyone had been in my house but the whole thing was still a little scary and worrisome.

Conversation turned to Tanya, we hadn't seen her for a while and were wondering how she was getting along with the divorce. "I'm not surprised he divorced her to be honest. Don't know how he put up with her for so long." said Becky

"Me either. I saw Mark in the cafe the other week with who I'm assuming is his new girlfriend." I told them "She seemed really nice, sweet, total opposite to Tanya. Mark looked like a different person, really happy, he always looked bloody miserable when he was with Tanya. Not surprised really she was always a right cold bitch with him. Always spoke to him like he was a piece of sh..."

"Oh, hi Tanya." interrupted Jill urgently. Looking up in alarm I followed her gaze to see Tanya standing at the side of us. Shit, how much had she heard? I readied myself for the onslaught but she just gave us a strange smile.

"Hello ladies, see you've all got drinks. Be right back." she said and flounced off to the bar.

"How long was she there? Did she hear me?" I asked Jill in a panic.

Jill shrugged her shoulders "I don't know, if she bottles you when she gets back from the bar then I guess she heard you."

Tanya returned from the bar with a drink, she was acting a little strange maybe but didn't seem to be angry. It seemed like we were in the clear. I dared to breathe again. "Cheers! Here's to cheating, cowardly soon to be ex husbands." she said smiling and raising her glass towards us.

"Cheers" we said back a little nervously.

"Oh and Happy Birthday Scarlett my lovely friend." she said raising her glass again in my direction.

"Erm, thanks Tanya." I said.

A little while later Neil joined us. I hadn't seen him for a few weeks as he'd been working away but we'd kept in touch by text message and the occasional phone call. All friendly and purely platonic of course. No flirtatious behaviour much to my disappointment. "Hope you ladies don't mind me popping by just wanted to wish Red a happy birthday" he said kissing me on my cheek and giving me a little box that had been beautifully gift wrapped.

"Of course not, please, join us." I indicated an empty seat next to mine. He sat down "Aww, you shouldn't have. Did you wrap this yourself?" I said taking the little box and giving him a big grin. I'd missed him.

"Don't be daft, I'm a man with man hands that are totally incapable of doing girlie shit like that! I got them to wrap it in the shop. It's only a little something but when I saw it I knew you had to have it."

It was a shame to spoil the gorgeous gift wrapping but I ripped it open to find the box contained a cute pair of silver stud earrings in the shape of paw prints. I'd had a pair just like them when I was younger and I'd been telling Neil how they'd been my most favourite thing in the whole wide world until I lost them, sure that one of my supposed friends had stolen them during a P.E. lesson at school one day and how gutted I'd been. I laughed, delighted at the thoughtfulness of the gift and the fact that he had remembered my birthday. I thanked him, kissing him on the cheek. Taking the new earrings out of the box I removed the earrings I was wearing and replaced them with the paw prints.

This was the first time Neil had met Tanya, I introduced them and he was an instant hit with her. The more drinks she had the more flirtatious she got with him, moving closer, fluttering her eyelashes at him, giggling inanely at everything he said and suggestively licking her lips every two minutes. I felt strangely possessive of him. Even though we weren't dating and our relationship up to that point had been purely platonic I didn't want superbitch Tanya getting her claws into him. Frankly she was rather pissing me off with her behaviour. Neil went to the bar to buy a round of drinks and Tanya took the opportunity to move sitting next to me in what had been Neil's seat so that when he came back she was sitting in between us.

"Thank you for the drink Neil." said Tanya, putting her hand firmly on his thigh as he sat back down.

"Erm, you're welcome." He replied, looking a little uncomfortable.

"So Scarlett," she said loudly, turning to me "how are things going with king dick Ben, the sex God?" She knew I hadn't told Neil about Ben, I could have cheerfully throttled the bitch.

"Not the time or place Tan." Becky said to

Tanya.

"Why not? She just loves to tell us about the amazing, fantastic sex she has with the man with the huge talented penis. How many orgasms did he give you on Sunday Scarlett?"

Neil was looking at me with a quizzical expression, I felt my face flush. "I am so sorry about this." I said.

"Who's Ben?" He asked

"He's just someone I'm having a bit of a casual thing with, friends with benefits kind of arrangement. Nothing serious."

"Bah!" slurred Tanya "She lurrrrves him!"

"Ah, I see. The complication. OK then. Well, I, erm, I think I'm going to get going" said Neil necking his drink and standing up.

"Don't go yet, the fun's just getting started" said Tanya pouting.

"I think I've had enough fun for one night. See ya." He said and, grabbing his coat, he made for the door.

I went after him "Neil, wait, can I please explain?"

"Nothing to explain here really is there Scarlett? See ya." He looked sad, and angry. I didn't blame him. Even though he had agreed to be just friends I knew he was hoping for more eventually and I should have been honest with him from the start. I wasn't sure why I hadn't been. I made my choice when Ben had asked me to go exclusive and I should have told Neil I was in a relationship but because I was so unsure about Ben I had been unfairly stringing Neil along, keeping him there as an option if things didn't work out with Ben. He had every right to be angry with me. What a horrible, selfish person I had been.

CHAPTER NINETEEN

The next morning I woke quite early, with a mixture of emotions. Excited about going away that afternoon with Ben but feeling sad and guilty about what had happened the night before with Neil. I showered, dressed and put my makeup on checking my watch every two minutes, butterflies in my tummy like a kid excited for Christmas. Ben had said he would pick me up at two and the minutes crawled by frustratingly. It got to around midday and I was a little concerned as he usually called or messaged me every morning but I hadn't heard from him yet that day. I sent him a quick message.

We still on track for 2? X

I waited half an hour but got no reply. I gave him a call but there was no answer, the phone just ringing and ringing until it went to the voicemail service. Puzzled, I sent another message.

Everything OK?

Pls call or msg x

One O'Clock came around, then two with no sign of Ben and no reply to my messages or return phone call. I rang him again but still got no answer, the call going to his voicemail once again. I left him a quick message asking if everything was OK and asking him to call me when he could. The day dragged on, no Ben, no call from Ben no messages from Ben. I was really concerned and more than a little disappointed. I considered driving over to see if he or Gina were home a couple of times but thought better of it. When it got to seven o'clock it was obvious we weren't going anywhere so I unpacked my overnight bag, flung my kinky knickers and hold up stockings back into the drawer, made myself a micro-ding curry from the freezer and opened a bottle of wine, disappointment sticking like a bone in my throat.

After a couple of glasses of wine to build up my courage I decided to ring Neil to try to explain the situation with Ben to him. I was nervous as I dialled his number, certain that he wouldn't answer or that he'd have blocked my number. It rang though and he answered, my stomach doing a little flip when I heard his voice. I was expecting him to sound angry but he just sounded a little sad and that was worse.

"I owe you an apology. I am so sorry I didn't tell

you about Ben." I said

"Hey, don't worry about it, it's fine, you don't owe me anything. It's not as if we're in a relationship, we've only had a couple of dates." he replied. The way he referred to our relationship, as if it was nothing special to him, cut through me like a knife.

"Yes, I know. But I should have told you."

"So what's the deal? Are things serious with this sex god Ben?" he asked

"I honestly don't know." I said

"Well listen, I really did like you, but that kind of open relationship thing isn't for me, sorry. So I guess we won't be going on any more dates." I felt another stab of the knife when I realised he had referred to liking me in the past tense.

"I understand" I did, but I felt very disappointed. "I really like you too. Can we still be friends?"

"Sure, OK, why not. I can do friends." He replied "No doubt I'll be seeing you in the pub from time to time, you can buy me a drink. Although don't be expecting me to have anything to do that weird friend of yours. She really isn't my type of people. To be honest, I'm a little scared of her."

I laughed, "You're on, the least I can do is buy you a drink. And truthfully, I'm a little scared of her too."

He laughed too "Thanks for ringing to explain. I'll see you soon. Take care."

"I am truly sorry about not being completely

honest with you." I said

"I know. Bye Red."

"Bye Neil" I said and hung up a little reluctantly. I wanted to carry on speaking to him but what else was there to say? I couldn't help feeling I had made the wrong choice here, but I couldn't give Ben up. I was addicted to him. All in all it had been a pretty shit twenty fours hours.

The buzz of my phone woke me early the next morning - a message off Ben at last -

```
I am so very sorry beautiful,
Gina got taken into hospital
yesterday morning and in all
the panic I forgot my phone.
Didn't get home until early
hours. I'll ring you shortly xxx
```

I didn't believe him. His phone was practically fused to his hand, he never, ever put that piece of bloody plastic down unless we were having sex. Something about this wasn't ringing true. Time to do a bit of cyber-stalking. I sat down at the kitchen table with a strong coffee and fired up my laptop. Logging into Facebook I did a search for him, hoping he had an account and that it was public. He did have an account but he hadn't posted anything for quite a while. I noticed Gina had liked a couple of his photos so I clicked on her name to take me to her profile. Bingo. She had a public profile, was quite a prolific poster and yesterday she had posted a photo of her and Ben windswept and laughing at the seaside with the dog. The feckin liar. I sat musing for a while about what to do. It was disappointment after disappointment, lie after lie with Ben. I was that fed up with it I couldn't even be bothered to be angry. He had blindsided me with his declaration of love, it had thrilled me, who didn't want to be loved? And I thought that I loved him but I was beginning to question that. Did I? Really? Apart from the odd meal we never did anything that wasn't about sex, most of our conversations centred around sex. He pushed me to try things I hadn't done before and that had excited me at first but when I actually sat and thought about it properly on that cold January morning I realised I was actually getting a little bored with the whole thing. The relationship didn't really have any substance.

A little while later my phone rang, Ben. I left it to go to voicemail, give him a taste of his own medicine I thought churlishly. Then, hating myself, I reached out, picked up the phone and called him back arranging for him to come over that night.

CHAPTER TWENTY

A couple of weeks went by and I was still feeling down and confused about my relationship with Ben. I thought about ending the relationship so many times and would make the decision to do so but then, when I saw him my resolve crumbled and I couldn't go through with it. When we were together I felt so loved and the sex was of course always amazing. The way he held me, I had just never felt like that in anyone's arms before. When I was with him I felt desirable, wanted and happy and safe. But when I wasn't with him I was forever questioning our relationship and my gut instincts were screaming at me not to trust him. I had arguments constantly in my head, he loves me... no he doesn't... it's all an act... no one can be that good an actor, he must love me... if he loves you he wouldn't do half the shit he does and he'd make more of an effort... and on and on and on. I was driving myself insane. I rang Jill and invited her over. “Impromptu Wine and Whine Wednesday?” She asked.

“Yes please” I said “I could really do with seeing a friendly face right now.”

“I’ll be there for eight” she promised and she was right on time with two bottles of my favourite White Zinfandel wine, a large box of Black Magic and a family sized bag of salt and vinegar crisps.

“I made an executive decision to incorporate Fuck the Diet Friday with Wine and Whine Wednesday this week. You sounded like you needed it.” she said, showing me the goodies. I smiled and hugged her, she and the goodies were just what the doctor ordered. Grabbing a couple of glasses we settled on the sofa.

“So” said Jill. She filled our glasses, passed one to me and we clinked them together “Cheers! What’s happenin’? Why so glum?”

“Ben” it was all I needed to say. She must have been sick of hearing it.

“Why? What’s up, what's he done now? Did you ever say anything to him about the birthday let down?” She asked. To add insult to injury, in addition to not showing up to take me away as promised, he had not even acknowledged my birthday. No card or gift, not even a cheap bunch of flowers from the garage. He had not even wished me a Happy Birthday.

“No. I felt a bit embarrassed about Facebook

stalking him and also I don't want him to know, that way I can carry on stalking him if I need to. I know, I know - I'm such a saddo. He really did let me down, I would have totally understood if it had been a genuine emergency but to lie about it. Then there's that bloody Lola who's constantly messaging him, he actually phoned her in front of me when we were in Blackpool, was very, very friendly and flirtatious during the call AND called her sexy bum which is what he fucking calls me."

"You're joking?! Shit. Sorry to state the obvious sweetie, but he's obviously still fucking her, or at least he wants to He's far too familiar with her for it to have been a one off casual thing, what? eight months ago? Is this the one who he said was a shit shag? The one who enjoys gang bangs at the swinger's parties?"

"Yeah. But she has lovely soft skin that he loved to massage apparently." I said sarcastically.

Jill rolled her eyes "Who keeps in touch with a shit shag for so long?"

"I know, and she's probably not the only one either. He's always messaging on the flirting groups and looking at the swingers hook up site. It makes me so bloody miserable."

"He's such a childish arsehole! I thought you said he wasn't on those sites any more, that he came off them when you fell out over it the other week?" After I'd seen him looking at the sites on his phone on more than one occasion and noticed him replying to messages I'd finally got up the courage to challenge him about it. He didn't think he was doing anything wrong because he said he wasn't hiding it from me, I disagreed and we'd fallen out about it. He had agreed to delete them all but he hadn't.

"Yeah, that's what he told me but he's still on them, I've seen them on his phone. I challenged him about it again and he offered to delete them, again. He assured me we are exclusive, he said he's not looking for anyone else, told me I'm everything he wants and needs blah, blah, blah, it's just that he just likes chatting with like-minded people and that's why he's still on the sites"

"Well that's the biggest load of bullshit I've ever heard. He's on there for one reason and one reason only. To stick his big knob in as many holes as possible. Feed his fucking weird perverted ego. Even if he said he'd delete them he wouldn't, he'd just hide it from you. He's a sneaky, lying fucktard. You need to end this madness, right now. You deserve so much better. What a greedy bastard he is. Doesn't just want to have his cake and eat it, he wants to eat everyone else's fucking cake too."

"I know, I know" I said, "but for some strange reason that I cannot figure out I'm so addicted to him. I've told him I don't want to see him any more after what happened in Blackpool but the idea of losing him completely makes me even sadder than all the shit he puts me through." I put my head in my hands, I felt like crying, my stomach churning with anxiety at the thought of never seeing him again. "I just don't know what to do." I said miserably.

"Scarlett, he needs to stay dumped, you need to move on. He's not good for your mental health. Can't you see all the lines he's been feeding you are just bullshit? He doesn't love you, if he did you would be enough for him. He wouldn't be doing all this fucking about. You have a great sex life, you are always there for him, you are so lovely and accommodating. You put up with and listen to him moan about his situation with Gina, but it's still not enough for him. Good God, no other woman would even put up with the Gina situation for long never mind all the other shit. They'd have sent him packing after he admitted they were still in a relationship. No matter how much you compromise and give him it will never be enough. Anyway you are way out of his league sweetie. Let him fuck all his nasty slappers, you are far too good for a man like that."

I knew what she was saying made sense. The relationship caused me a lot of pain and heartache. I was forever wondering where he was and who he was with. I knew he lied to me often. I had no issue whatsoever about his relationship with Gina even though he had misled me about that, I didn't even mind him being in contact with some of his ex's but the idea of him still having sex with other women was something I just couldn't handle.

Ben and I had been to Blackpool the weekend before. “Let’s go for a romantic weekend away to make up for your birthday” he’d suggested. I’d readily agreed, we didn’t get to spend much time together so the idea of a weekend away with him was fantastic. I was disappointed when he rang me Friday afternoon “Sorry, babe, something’s come up. Can’t go today. Will definitely go tomorrow. Will try to get over to you early. Love you.” He didn’t elaborate on what had come up and I didn’t ask him. Probably another woman.

He didn’t pick me up until 6pm on Saturday evening and ended up dropping me back off at 10am Sunday morning, so hardly a weekend, not even a full 24hrs. And the fact that he took me to a swingers club was hardly what you would call romantic. I booked us into a B&B on the drive over as he had neglected to book anywhere. There wasn’t much availability anywhere decent as it was last minute but luckily it was out of season and I did manage to find a lovely little place, clean and newly decorated with a very friendly landlady. It was almost eight o’clock when we arrived so we left our bags in the room and then headed straight out for something to eat. The trendy steak restaurant I had been hoping for was fully booked so we ended up at a pizza place. Although I was a little disappointed to miss out on the nice restaurant it wasn’t really an issue. I love food but I'm not a food snob, just feed me and I'm happy. I was determined to make the most of this rare treat of having Ben all to myself for the whole night.

The evening began to go rapidly downhill when we arrived at the restaurant. He was constantly on his phone as usual the ignorant swine, only putting it down when the food arrived. Whilst we were eating he made the mistake of leaving his phone face up on the table, usually he was quite secretive with it, placing it face down and on silent. A message popped up, I couldn't help but look. Fucking Lola. Again. He had been getting messages from her for a couple of weeks now, although I hadn't been deliberately looking I had noticed them pop up on his home screen from time to time.

"Ah." he flustered, noticing me looking at his phone "Erm... you remember me telling you about Lola? She's seeing someone who's supposed to be in MI5 or something. It's all a bit weird, he won't give her his number or any contact information, says he can't because of his job. He contacts her through the swingers group. He's always travelling all over the place. He's very secretive, I think he's a bit dodgy."

Like someone else I know I thought "What a crock of shit." I said "As if he'd tell her he was a spy! More likely he's married."

"Yeah, probably" he agreed. He then amazed me by picking up his phone and calling her. "Hiya sexy bum, how are you?" He said smiling when she answered. The same greeting he used with me. The exact same inflection in his voice. I was bloody livid. How fucking rude! "I'm in Blackpool with the sexy Scarlett, we're going to Bonkers." He listened for a moment and gave a little laugh "No, no, not yet" he looked at me, winked and smiled "she's not agreed to a threesome yet but I'll work on her."

What the fuck? My temper went from livid to raging to apocalyptic in 0.3 seconds. I couldn't sit there and listen to him chatting intimately with this woman. And as for a threesome? I doubt I'd ever have a threesome with another woman anyway and even if I did consider it there was not a cat in hells chance it would ever be with her. How I didn't explode in anger I don't know. I stood up and went to find the toilet before I did something nasty to him with the pizza cutter. Coming back from the toilet via a double vodka at the bar, I managed to calm myself down from nuclear, to somewhat calm albeit with a "Here's Johnny!" homicidal smile fixed to my face. He was just ending the call with a "See ya later gorgeous" as I approached the table and sat down. He looked at me "Everything OK beautiful?" he enquired smiling his stupid crooked grin at me. The one I used to find so endearing.

We all know men can be a bit thick when it comes to women so here's a heads up just for them. If you ask a woman if she's ok and she says "I'm fine" then the likelihood is she isn't fine. Especially if she has shown signs of being in a bad mood. Some clues that she may be in a bad mood may include but are not limited to - stomping around, throwing things, slamming doors, muttering to herself, repeatedly ramming the vacuum cleaner into your shins whilst you're sat playing on your video games, huffing or giving you the stare of death. If she says "I'm fine" and emphasises the word fine then it's probably still safe to be near her but you may have to up your game and make her a cup of tea or something. If the "I'm FINE!" is shouty then, even if you have no idea what you have done wrong, you will probably need to apologise with flowers, chocolates, jewellery etc. But, if she says it without moving her lips and with a strange, scary little smile then trust me you are in deep shit and you need to make yourself scarce for a while if you value your life.

"Oh I'm fine" I spat at Ben through gritted teeth, sitting on my hands so I wouldn't be tempted to pick something up and throw it at his stupid thick skull "just peachy honey. Couldn't be better." Why oh why am I putting up with this bullshit I thought? It just wasn't worth it. He was definitely seeing her. I now had no doubt in my mind about that. He continued to smile at me, still totally oblivious to my homicidal mood.

We went from the restaurant to the club via an off licence where I purchased a half bottle of vodka. Ben had explained to me that the club wasn't licensed to sell alcohol but you could take your own in with you. You left your bottle at the bar and just paid for the mixer. I was tempted by a full bottle but I knew the mood I was in, I would just neck it all rather too quickly and end up in a right old state. Not a great idea when I needed to have my wits at least partially about me when we were in the club. We hadn't been to this one before, or at least I hadn't, Ben of course had been before with other women. He'd been to more or less every club in the North West and quite a few in the rest of the country besides. Shagging was his favourite hobby after all.

CHAPTER TWENTY ONE

I managed to outwardly calm myself down somewhat on the taxi journey to the club but I was still seething inside. Totally oblivious to my dangerous mood Ben chatted away, excitedly telling me about Bonkers and some of the outrageous nights he had had in there. I was finding the initial excitement I'd felt about the clubs waning, the novelty was wearing off. His stories were beginning to bore me.

We arrived at the club. It was OK, much the same as the one nearer home but with a slightly different layout. Although I wasn't really feeling it I got dressed up in some sexy new black lacy underwear and stockings that I had bought especially for the occasion. Maybe I could find some young, well-hung hunk of man to flirt with in front of Ben, that would bloody well serve him right I thought. We got a drink and went to sit down for a while in an area that had leather sofas, a pool table and a couple of big tv's showing the obligatory dodgy porn. We hadn't been sitting there long when a couple came into the room. They both had the stare-eyed look of a cocaine high. The man sat on the coffee table in front of us, the woman undoing the towel he was wearing and grabbing his cock. She smiled and winked at me "want to help me out with my hubby's dick?" She enquired kneeling in front of him, giving his dick a few slow strokes and then leisurely sucking it. "It tastes really, really good" she informed me, licking her lips.

"Erm, no thanks." I said not knowing quite where to look "Thanks for the offer. I'm a bit new to this so just sussing it all out at the moment."

"Ah, OK, is this your first time?" She asked whilst she continued to pleasure her husband. "You look really good, not at all like a newbie. Love your gear."

"Thank you." I said, wondering what a newbie normally looked like.

She continued to slurp on her hubbies man-lolly for a few minutes whilst I looked in the other direction. Finally she finished and they both stood up.

"If you want to join us for some fun later, come and find us." She said with another lewd wink, then taking her husband's hand they sauntered off. Ben wasn't very impressed with their antics, commented that they were rude and that they had broken swingers etiquette. Probably sulking because he hadn't been included in the invite.

A few minutes later a young girl, probably in her early twenties came into the room wearing nothing but a thong and a smile. She was a very big girl but carried herself with a confidence I wish I'd had when I was her age, wish I had now actually. A skinny, spotty boy was with her wearing a towel around his scrawny waist. They started a game of pool. Ben was leant forward, watching her intently "Look at that, that's sexy" he commented, tongue hanging out, practically drooling as she bent over the table to take a shot giving us a view of her enormous cellulite ridden arse in its full glory.

Really? I thought. Wow! She was like less than half his age, seriously obese, in need of a good wash with lank, greasy, badly dyed yellow hair that had four inches of dark roots. Her bitten fingernails had badly chipped black varnish and the teeth she did have left were rotten. He was perving over that?

I looked at him with a puzzled expression. "Are you kidding? You honestly find that attractive?" I asked him.

"Yeah" he replied "look how confident she is. I bet she's an amazing fuck."

Jesus! I was learning a lot about Ben today that I really didn't want to know. "Would you take one for the team?" he asked, indicating the spotty youth.

"What? Would I fuck him whilst you fucked her you mean?" I asked appalled.

"Yeah" he said in all seriousness.

"Not a frigging chance mate. Ever!" I was outraged and disgusted.

Just then a handsome black guy came sauntering in wearing nothing but a towel which was casually thrown over his right shoulder. He had an amazing body and a very large cock. Even bigger than Ben's. He looked over and smiled at me. I smiled back. "Now, I'd take one for the team if he was a member of the other side." I commented to Ben.

He didn't look the least bit impressed. "Come on" he said moodily, standing up and offering me his hand "I'll show you the rest of the club." Just as I was beginning to enjoy the view, spoilsport!

He showed me the private and group sex rooms which were upstairs. Again they consisted mostly of mirrors and PVC covered thick mattresses. All the PVC was black here and very shiny. It looked wet. There was a room with a small assortment of whips, handcuffs and chains but it was a bit of a poor effort in comparison to the dungeon at the other club we'd been to. All the rooms were unoccupied, no shagging going on yet but it was still early. We went back downstairs to the wet area and got into the Jacuzzi. There was another couple in there, very friendly who introduced themselves as Trisha and Simon. We chatted for a while, it should have felt weird, I suppose, meeting new people whilst naked in a jacuzzi, could you imagine everyone just turning up at the pub naked? But it didn't feel weird at all in the context of the venue. They were really lovely, about ten years younger than us, they had seven children and had been married for twelve years.

"I've been swinging since I was about nineteen" Trisha told me "I met Simon when I was twenty one. He was a right old tart and I knew he'd never be faithful so I told him we could carry on swinging, but only together so I knew who he was with and so I could have my fun too." I was blown away by the fact that they had managed to have seven kids and still have such an active sex life.

Whilst I was talking to Trisha I noticed Ben keep standing up in the jacuzzi muttering something about it being too warm. It wasn't. His dick was just above the water line and he made a great show of putting his hands behind his back, pushing his hips out as if his lower back was hurting him. He didn't fool anyone with this act, least of all me, what he was really doing was showing off the size of his tackle saying "Look at my huge dick". Despite his best efforts Trisha took no notice of him, I guess she had seen her fair share of big knobs over the years and was not overly impressed by Ben's. Finally, realising no one was taking any notice of him or his big dick he gave up and asked me if I would like another drink. "Yes please." I said. He made a great drama of climbing out of the jacuzzi, pausing on the steps to give Trisha a dazzling smile and a good eyeful of his manhood then wrapped a towel around his waist and walked off in the direction of the bar.

A few minutes later, still chatting to Trisha I glanced up and spied him standing at the side of the bar chatting intently to the fat young girl we had seen in the pool room. I watched as he whispered something in her ear, she laughed at him and nodded. Fuming I sat and stared unbelievingly as he started to fondle her fat tits and then raged even more when she reached inside his towel to feel his dick. What the fuck was he doing?

Trisha followed my stare "This is not really your thing this is it?" She remarked "how long have you two been together?"

"About five months" I replied.

"He told you he was a swinger when you met?" She questioned.

"He told me he *used* to be. He keeps trying to get me into it and no offence, but no, it's not my thing." It had taken me until that moment to realise for sure but no, it definitely wasn't.

"No offence taken, each to their own. Look, he's not going to change. Take my advice best to call it a day, you'll just end up getting hurt. Men like that, they can't help themselves."

"He says he loves me, I guess I just don't understand all this wanting sex with other women."

"It is just sex, he probably does love you if he says he does. We love each other like crazy" said Trisha nodding at her husband who was openly flirting with another woman who had just got into the pool "but we like sex with other people too."

"How do you cope with the jealousy?" I asked

She shrugged "I guess we just don't do jealousy."

"But I just can't believe he finds that attractive." I said, indicating the girl who's enormous tits he was enthusiastically still feeling.

"Well I must admit, present company excepted, he's obviously got low standards. A lot of men like big women, but she's just minging. She comes here a lot, shags everyone who's up for it. Looks like he's a quantity over quality swinger - any hole's a goal! I hope you use condoms!"

I was at a loss over what to do. I was absolutely livid with him, seething with jealousy and just wanted to go home but I was a bit drunk, was miles away from home, it was too late for trains and there was no way I could afford to waste the money on a taxi all that way it would cost a fortune. I could ask him to drive me home I suppose, he didn't drink so he was sober but I really didn't want to sit in a car with him for an hour and a half.

I got out of the jacuzzi, wrapped a towel around myself and sat on one of the loungers near the pool waiting for Ben. A few minutes later he came wandering over with my drink looking very pleased with himself. He went to hand me the drink but I couldn't bring myself to touch it knowing the skanky body his hands had just been all over. I told him to put it on the table next to the lounger.

"You OK babe?" He questioned. Even the dumbest of the dumb couldn't help to pick up on the fact that I was not in the best of moods.

"Nope." I replied "I want to go."

"But the night's just getting started."

The night had been a disaster from the very beginning. I couldn't honestly see it getting any better. "OK, tell you what. I'll go, you stay. But you do not come back to the same room as me. I will leave your stuff in reception. I'll get a train home tomorrow."

"What, but why?" He seemed genuinely perplexed.

"Enjoyed yourself feeling that dirty bitch up did you? Was she impressed with the size of your cock? Planning to fuck her later?"

"No, no, it's not like that. It was just a bit of fun. It was just a little feel. No sex."

"Sorry, but not acceptable. We agreed no messing with anyone else until I decided if it was for me or not. Well I've come to the conclusion that it definitely isn't for me and I want to go." I got up and went upstairs to get dressed. Ben dithered for a moment but then made the smart decision to follow me.

We got back to the bed and breakfast, got undressed and into bed, me turning my back on him and lying as close to the edge of the bed as far away from him as I could possibly manage. The thought of him touching me right then made me feel sick.

"I'm sorry babe," he said, "I'm so used to being with partners who are swingers that I forget. I promise, it won't happen again." He snuggled into me and put his arm around my waist.

"No, it won't happen again." I agreed, there was no way I was ever going to a club with him again, I wasn't even sure I wanted to carry on seeing him. My eyes had really been opened wide that night. "Get off me. Do NOT touch me. Sleep at the other side of the bed or go get another fucking room."

The next morning things were very strained between us. I was awake, showered, dressed and ready to go for 8am which was almost unknown for me. I am most definitely not normally a morning person. Ben drove me home mostly in silence giving up on trying to get me to converse with him when I would only answer with the occasional yeah, no or mmm. We arrived at my house and I got out of the car, grabbed my bag from the back seat and slammed the doors closed. Ben had also got out of the car. "Bye" I said to him, he was not coming into the house. I didn't want him there. He walked over to me and tried to kiss me but I turned my face away so he only got my cheek and then walked down my path. I went into the house and closed the door. Looking out of the window I could see he was still standing beside the car outside the house. Maybe he was debating whether or not he should try to come in and to talk to me, but in the end he must have thought better of it and he eventually drove off.

I sat quietly on the sofa for a while contemplating what had happened the night before. Was I over reacting? I didn't think so, I was miserable about the whole thing. In fact I realised miserable and anxious had seemed to be my default setting ever since I had started seeing Ben. I decided that was it, this was never going to work, we lived in different worlds, our brains didn't work the same. I couldn't help my jealousy and I couldn't stand the thought of him being with other women. It was making me miserable. Whenever I wasn't with him all I could think about was who he was with what he was doing, there was no trust there. I could do friends with benefits or an open relationship but I couldn't do it with a man I had strong feelings for perhaps even loved. He was what he was and he would never change. I knew that now but it would be too hard for me to make allowances for it because I just didn't get it. I didn't understand the need to have sex just for the sake of it with other people when you had a perfectly willing, loving partner already. Being deceived into being in a polyamorous relationship, knowing he loved someone else and had a life and a home with her was bad enough but knowing he was probably still casually putting it about and lying to me about it was more than I could cope with. I had no problem whatsoever with people doing whatever they wanted as long as it was ethical, legal and consensual and I am far from a prude but this lifestyle just wasn't for me.

I made my decision and called him. "I'm sorry, this isn't for me Ben." I said when he answered " I don't want to see you anymore." He tried to convince me not to end if of course, promised me he would change etc. But we both knew he wouldn't. My heart was broken but it was for the best.

CHAPTER TWENTY TWO

It had been about two weeks since I'd last seen Ben, I was missing him like crazy or maybe I was just missing the sex, either way I was miserable. I got the occasional text asking if we could try again, promising me he would change but I managed to remain resolute, it just wasn't worth the heartache.

Friday night and I was in my usual Friday night place, down the pub. There was only me and Becky out that night, Jill was away for the week-end with Emma, the girl she had met at Shona's Christmas party. They'd been together for almost three months now, a record for Jill and they ap-peared to be very happy. We hadn't seen anything of Tanya the superbitch since she'd gone off on one in the pub a few weeks earlier on my birthday telling Neil about Ben and it was Julie's weekend to be unfairly tortured by the living nightmares that were her two boys.

I went to the bar and was delighted to bump into Neil. Although we had kept in touch with the occasional polite 'how are you' type text message I hadn't seen him for a few weeks. I had considered ringing him a couple of times to tell him things were over with Ben and ask if he fancied going on a date but then had decided against it. I was far too fragile to cope with rejection right then if he turned me down, which he probably would do and was no more than I deserved with the awful way I had treated him. When I saw him I realised just how much I had missed him and I was disappointed and a little jealous to see he was with a glamorous looking blonde that I had never seen before. We exchanged hellos and he introduced us. "Red, this is Cheryl, Cheryl my friend Scarlett."

"Hello Scarlett." Cheryl breathed in a Marilyn Monroe style voice which just had to be as fake as her nails "Love your name."

"Thanks, erm.. love your hair." Truthfully, I didn't, it was bleached to within an inch of its life and huge. She looked like she'd dropped out of an eighties American soap or nicked a drag queen's wig.

"Thanks, well I do own a hair salon so it just wouldn't do if I had rubbish hair" she giggled patting her frizzy disaster and looking pointedly at my rubbish hair "Here, I'm sure I could do something with yours." she said, opening her handbag and handing me a business card.

"Thanks" I said through gritted teeth whilst Neil stood looking at his feet trying not to laugh.

"Why do people call you Red?" She asked in that breathy little voice that I'm sure she thought sexy but just made her sound dumb.

"Oh not people, just Neil" I replied "it's his nickname for me."

She didn't like that he had a nickname for me, pouting she asked him why he called me that.

"Because her name's Scarlett. It's a shade of red." He explained.

"Oh well that's just silly, if you want a nickname you should just shorten Scarlett, to Scar. Although, wait, that's not very nice is it? What about Lottie? Yes! We should call you Lottie! It's cute." she giggled.

No, I thought, you really shouldn't. "I don't think I look like a Lottie really." I said.

"No." agreed Neil laughing "She looks more like a Scar than a Lottie!" Charming! "But I think I'll stick to Red." He winked at me. Cheryl really didn't like that either. Sticking out her bottom lip she asked him what time the table was booked for and looked at her watch.

"Have fun you two lovebirds." I said and went to rejoin Becky at our table.

I sat back down with Becky, handed over her drink and we both looked at Cheryl who was busy checking her perfect makeup in a compact mirror, watching as she took out a lip gloss and re-coated her already perfectly shiny pout. Neil looked over and I mouthed "what the fuck?" to him, he just shrugged his shoulders at me looking amused with himself. Cheryl disappeared to the loo and Neil texted me -

What do you think of Cheryl?

Miss candy floss hair?

Aww she's lovely x

Sorry mate, if you're trying to make me jealous you'll have to do better than that!!!!

Hahaha x

Trying to keep my mind off Ben I went on a couple of dates. Both disasters. Julie had set me up on a blind date with someone she worked with called Simon. I'd had high hopes after Julie told me how nice he was. He did have a lovely personality and was filthy rich with a high flying career in banking, a great catch but truthfully he had a very unfortunate face, the kind of face that would have really suited a balaclava. I just didn't fancy him.

"What did you think of Simon then? Nice guy isn't he? He really likes you." said Julie when I next saw her.

"He is lovely," I agreed "just not for me. He has a bit of a strange face."

"Well, no he's not the most handsome of men but looks aren't everything."

"His hair hangs over his face like a pair of curtains." I pointed out

"He can always get a haircut."

"He was wearing a pink shirt and navy tie, with formal trousers. For a casual drink. He looked like he was going to a wedding."

"At least he was smart. You could always go clothes shopping with him." she suggested.

"Seriously, he's not for me. I'm sure there's a woman out there, other than his mum that will love him and his strange face but he's not me, sorry!"

I also arranged a Tinder date with a guy named Greg who had the strangest walk - he'd either just been circumcised, had enormous bollocks or was cursed with rickets and was one of the most boring people I had ever met in my whole life. I was completely underwhelmed by him. It was very, very difficult to stay awake, the number of times I yawned was embarrassing. I had to apologise several times and make up some obscure medical condition to account for it. Arriving home after the date with Greg I opened a bottle of wine and drank the lot. I was pissed off, I just couldn't be arsed going through all this dating shit again. My phone buzzed, Ben -

Missing you babe, please
will you give me one more
chance? X

I hardly thought about it, I was horny, I missed him, I was drunk. I was sick of dating already. Bad combination, very bad. I replied -

Come over

He came over, we made love. He held me close and told me how much he had missed me and how much he loved me. I didn't believe him anymore but I listened to it anyway breathing in his lovely smell and letting myself be taken in by the fantasy of it all. He left before midnight. I hated myself for being so weak.

CHAPTER TWENTY THREE

The clocks went forward, April arrived bringing with it the sunshine and showers. The relationship with Ben was back to the stomach churning anxiety ridden confusion that it was previously. He had given up on asking me to go to the swingers clubs with him and I pretended that I believed he loved me and tried to forget that he was more than likely shagging other women. I was fucking miserable truth be told but the sex was still amazing and I allowed myself to get lost in the fantasy and lies of love for those few hours a week I spent with him.

Life carried on as normal for a while. I told the girls I was seeing Ben again. They voiced their disapproval at first but then gave up trying to tell me he was bad for me. It was something I knew already. I just stopped talking to them about him, I knew they were sick of hearing about it, I would have been too. I was burying my head in the sand, I knew he was a liar and probably a cheat but I couldn't help myself.

I stayed friendly with Neil, we messaged often and spoke on the phone occasionally. Surprisingly he and candy floss hair Cheryl were dating on a regular basis and I found myself imagining their meal and drinks dates, trips to the cinema and spending nights together. I was jealous of her. I found myself thinking often about what could have been with Neil if it hadn't been for my infatuation with Ben.

The second week in April, I was hosting Wine and Whine Wednesday. Jill, Becky, Julie and Shona came round. These women I have so much love for, they keep me sane. Well, sane-ish.

"I've been thinking" announced Julie "I'm going to have a go of the dating app things"

We laughed. It's the last thing we would have thought Julie would do "I'm serious" she said "I'd like to have sex again before I retire."

"Come on then, let's get you set up." I said. We spent an hilarious evening setting up her profiles and matching her with some seriously unsuitable men.

Part way through the evening I received a random text off Ben -

I love you Charlotte xx

What the fuck? Charlotte???

The name is SCARLETT!!!
unless of course
you've sent this to the
wrong woman

OMG, I am such an idiot!
So sorry, I voiced typed it
and it has misunderstood
Scarlett. Must be my accent.
Forgive me beautiful xx

I showed the text to the girls. Please get rid of him, they implored of me. He's just no good for you, he's a player, you can do better, etc, etc. I thought about it and was shocked to find the thought of not seeing him any more wasn't quite as traumatic as it had previously been. Even the thought of sex with him didn't excite me as much as it once did.

"What does he look like, this Ben? Are we ever going to meet him?" asked Becky

I picked up my phone again and showed them a picture Ben had sent me a few days earlier of him with his dog.

"Which one's the dog?" asked Jill.

"That's not very nice!" I said laughing a bit "OK, he's not the best looking guy but he's amazing in bed."

"Good job he's got a big dick, otherwise he'd never get any sex." remarked Julie "Right, back to Plenty of Fish, ooh four new messages, lets see if any of them can spell, and how many of them look like they could be my grandad!"

It was the following Sunday when I saw Ben again. By this point I had given up on the pretence or hope of anything resembling a normal relationship with him and accepted that I was just his bit on the side. That's all I was. Probably one of a few. We were just having an affair, his life was with someone else. He told me he loved me often but deep down I knew they were only words that tripped easily off his tongue and they didn't really mean anything. He stopped taking me out for meals, we never went anywhere but the bedroom any more. I had never met any of his friends, he had no interest in meeting mine. I felt like I was like a dirty secret. He fucked me, snoozed for a couple of hours then he went home. We probably only actually spent about three hours a week awake with each other. Even the sex was becoming a bit predictable, the initial bit of Sub / Dom play had kind of petered out much to my disappointment, replaced by hints about group sex and watching me have sex with other men which I definately wasn't up for and really didn't understand. He tried to explain "It's the sting, watching you with someone else and then punishing you for it later." Ah, OK, so he basically got his rocks off by pimping me out for free to other men whilst he watched and then I'd get some form of punishment for doing what he wanted me to do. Right! Nope, I still didn't get it. I told him I still didn't understand but he just shrugged and told me he thought there was something wrong with how his brain was wired up. Yep, I'd have to agree with that. He told me most men fantasize about weird shit like that but he was actually brave enough to act on his fantasies.

I wondered about Gina, whether her brain was wired up wrong too, if the knowledge of him being with other women got her hot or if she just put up with it because she was ill and had no place else to go. I knew that if I wanted to stay sane I had no choice other than to end this destructive relationship but I was firmly stuck in a hole and had no idea how I was going to climb out of it. The sex that Sunday night was great as it usually was. Loving, tactile, horny. That was the problem, that was what I was addicted to.

After sex Ben picked up his phone, checking for messages as he usually did. I glanced over noticing he had a notification and saw him click on it opening a link to a group chat called 'NW Big Boys'. Turning the phone away slightly so I was unable to see he quickly typed something then put it down at the side of the bed. After a few minutes he fell asleep as usual. I lay there next to him watching him snoring wondering for the millionth time how on earth this man had such a hold over me and what it was he had texted to 'NW Big Boys'.

He had face recognition security on his phone but once, when he had been at my house, his battery had completely died. After he had charged it up he'd had to input his code. I had surreptitiously watched as he typed it in pretending to look at something on my iPad. It had looked like 220373, his birthday, not very secure or imaginative and I had filed the information away for future use. I didn't like to spy on him but I really didn't trust him and the whole thing was driving me insane. I had to find out whether what I suspected about him was true or if I was being unfair to him with my distrust.

Once I was sure he was fast asleep I crept silently around to his side of the bed and picked up his phone taking it into the bathroom. My heart was beating fast, my mouth dry and my hands shook a little as I typed in the code. I wasn't cut out to be a spy. Bingo! The phone unlocked and his home screen came up. I paused for a moment, it felt wrong this invasion of privacy, I'm usually a trusting person, but I had to know. The Big Boys group had been on QuiKChat so I opened the app, cursing when it asked me for another passcode. It was seven digits. I thought about it for a moment then holding my breath I typed in BEN2203, amazed when it worked. No imagination that man nor overly concerned about security. I began scrolling through the group posts, shocked and disgusted by what I was seeing. I soon came across Ben's most recent post, a text. His username was 'BigBenTen' which made me roll my eyes. His text read -

At the lovely Scarlett's,
just had very
satisfactory sex ending
with an excellent blowjob.
She's a great fuck,
so accommodating,
shame she's so vanilla.

'FuckBuddy27' had replied -

Doing well with that one,
don't know how you've kept
her interested for so long.
Have fucked her up the arse
yet brother?

She's totally seduced by
the lovecraft!
No anal yet, she's worried about
staying anal retentive haha
but I'm working on it.
Get plenty of that off Lola

What the hell? Were all of our sexual exploits broadcast to this group? And here was the proof, he was definitely still fucking Lola. Scrolling through the posts it became apparent that this was some sort of sick, sexual conquests bragging group. There were even photos and videos on there of naked women and men and women performing sex acts. I felt sick. Ben had suggested to me a few times that we take photos or make videos and I was so glad I had always said no. I was always too worried about revenge porn after reading a couple of articles about it. I heard him cough from the bedroom and shut the phone down quickly, worried that he would wake up and find it gone. I opened the door a crack and listened, relieved to hear that he was still snoring softly. I had lost my bravery for now though and I'd seen enough. Creeping back into the bedroom I put his phone back where I had found it. Standing at the side of the bed I looked at his peaceful sleeping face for a while, barely resisting the urge to smash his lying skull in. Well, I had my proof now, he'd never loved me, it was all lies, he'd manipulated me so I'd keep having sex with him. Deep down I'd always suspected this of course, now I had irrefutable proof it was time I accepted it.

I went downstairs, there was no way I could get back into bed with him after what I had just seen. Just looking at him made my skin crawl. In the kitchen I made a cup of tea and sat at the table contemplating what to do. So many emotions ran through me, top of which was rage, but also sadness and disappointment. I felt so humiliated. I couldn't believe I had put up with all his shit, forgiving him all the time because I thought we'd had something special when it had all been a lie. Time and time again he'd let me down and time and time again I'd forgiven him and taken him back believing he actually cared for me when all along I'd been nothing more than another sexual conquest for him. I must be a special kind of stupid to have not seen him for what he really was. Actually I realised I did, I'd always really known exactly what he was and I had chosen to ignore it which made me even more super specially stupid. Was I really that desperate to feel loved?

I heard the alarm sound on his phone upstairs and looked up at the clock, 11.45. He was like bloody Cinderella always buggering off before midnight. I could hear him moving around upstairs then I heard the toilet flush followed by the sound of him coming down the stairs. He came into the kitchen.

"There you are! What are you doing down here?" He asked.

"Oh, couldn't sleep, decided I needed a cup of tea." I said lifting my cup, amazed at how civil I sounded.

He smiled. "Got to run, it was amazing as usual babe. Speak tomorrow."

"Yep" I replied "Amazing. Ten out of ten." He kissed me and then turned to leave. "Don't forget your glass slippers." I said under my breath as he headed towards the door.

He turned back "Did you say something?"

"Nope" I said smiling sweetly at him "Bye honey, drive carefully."

"Bye, love you." He said

Yeah, of course you do. Lying, cheating fucktard.

CHAPTER TWENTY FOUR

The next evening around nine there was a knock at my door. I opened it surprised to find Julie standing there, looking a little upset.

"Oh! Hi Julie, come in. Is everything OK? Where are the boys?" I said

"They're with Martha, I had to wait until they were both asleep and then bribe her with a bottle of brandy and my new Jamie Oliver cook book, promise I wouldn't be longer than an hour and half and that I would go home immediately if they woke up." Martha was Julie's next door neighbour, a recently retired headteacher who had spent sixteen years as the head of a school for problem kids that had been kicked out of mainstream school, but even she couldn't cope with Julie's monsters.

We went into the living room and sat down. I was having a glass of wine and offered her one but she declined asking for a cup of tea instead as she was driving.

"What's up Jules?" I questioned as we waited for the kettle to boil "you don't seem to be your usual self."

"Well, it's just that, erm... well there's no easy way of saying it really. Sorry but Ben's still active on the dating sites. I wasn't sure it was him at first but when I looked at his profile pictures the one you showed me the other day, the one with his dog? That was on there."

My heart sunk. I already had evidence that I had been right not to trust him, that he was screwing around still and this was further proof of his lies "Maybe he's just not got round to removing his profiles?" I said, inexplicably still wanting to give him the benefit of doubt even after seeing what he had put on that awful chat group yesterday. Why on earth was I trying to defend him? Why?

"I thought maybe that was the case at first but he was actually online and, I'm sorry but he messaged me."

"Did he? What did he say?"

She picked up her phone, opened the dating app and showed me the message -

Hello, I hope you don't mind me messaging but your profile and your beautiful picture caught my eye. I know you are way out of my league but if you would like to chat sometime it would make me very happy. If not I understand and wish you the very best with your search for love. Take care gorgeous xx

And there it was. The cure. This, coupled with discovering what he had put on the NW Big Boys group last night, totally and immediately cured my insane addiction to him. It was like a bucket of iced water poured over my head followed by a hearty slap across the cheeks and a firm kick up the arse. The message was practically identical to the first message he had sent to me, the fucking gobshite. But what to do about it? My immediate reaction was to ring him and give him a few choice words telling him exactly what I thought of him but no, after all the shit he'd put me through he deserved a much better punishment than that.

"Have you replied?" I asked

"No, I've not done anything yet. I thought I would come and tell you immediately"

"Don't respond for now." I told Julie "Let me have a think about what to do."

"OK" she said "I am so sorry, I know we all think he's no good for you but I know you really like him."

"You've nothing to be sorry about. And yes, I did really like him but truthfully I've always had my doubts about him, more so recently. I was thinking of ending it anyway." I explained to her what I had seen on his phone the night before.

"That is bloody disgusting." She said, shocked

"How fucking disrespectful. Are you OK?"

"I'm mostly angry and a little upset and of course totally humiliated but I'll be fine. Don't worry about me. I'll call you later when I've decided what to do."

After she left I sat seething with anger for a while, I couldn't believe I had been played so well by that smarmy, sex pest. But what should I do about the situation? Ben had not yet met any of my friends hence the fact that he hadn't realised I knew Julie. She lived in a different town to me so perhaps he thought he was safe messaging her and that it wouldn't be someone I would find out about. I knew now it was over, for definite and for good, no going back this time. Surprisingly I actually found I felt relieved about it and couldn't wait to tell him we were finished but I wasn't letting him off the hook easily after all his lies and the way he had been using and playing me all along. I began to formulate a plan.

I continued to message and talk to him the same as usual as if everything was OK. I was supposed to be seeing him on Thursday but I made my excuses the day before saying I was poorly with a migraine and asked if we could leave it until Sunday. He made some insincere noises saying he hoped I felt better soon, told me he loved me (how easily the lie rolled off his tongue) and said he'd look forward to seeing me on Sunday.

In the meantime my plan for revenge was coming along nicely. Julie had given me her account password for OK Cupid and I was conversing with Ben pretending to be her, egging him along and pretending to be very interested in him. Jill also set up an account, liking Ben's profile to see if he would message her. "Jesus, look at all these perverts. I'm so glad I'm a lesbian, men are so disrespectful." She said reading through some of the messages she had received telling her in great detail, complete with bad spelling and punctuation, what they wanted to do to her and asking for naked pictures for their wank banks. How come the most perverted were also the most illiterate? Anyway, we didn't have to wait long for Ben, day two, he bit - sending Jill the exact identical message he had sent to Julie. "Haha! Gotcha!" she said rubbing her hands together "King Dick - you are going down!"

On Friday, I met Julie, Jill and Becky in the pub where we discussed the action points of our plan. The flirty chat had been going well and he'd arranged dates with both Julie (me) and Jill for early the following week. I had played it a little demurely pretending to be Julie but Jill had gone fully to town on him, playing to his sex addict side saying she was into swinging, was bi-sexual and a bit of a nymphomaniac. She had been inserting lots of not so subtle innuendo into their conversations. He had sent her the short video of his penis, the same one he had sent to me, and she had pretended to be impressed telling him that she couldn't wait to ride it and she had a friend who would be more than happy to help her out with it too. The more outrageous she got with her messages the more excited he got. I'm willing to bet he was finding it very difficult to concentrate at work that week. We had him where we wanted him. Time to go into phase two.

I messaged him to cancel our Sunday arrangement -

Hiya, sorry I'm still not feeling very well, I think it could be a bit of flu and you can't risk taking that home to Gina with her illness. Can we rearrange Sunday? Xx

My phone pinged back straight away with a sad face emoji -

Sorry you're still not feeling so well beautiful. Shall I ring you? x

Not now, going to have an early night x

Speak 2morrow x

OK sexy bum, sleep well xxx

It was less than two minutes before Jill's phone pinged, a message on the dating site. Ben -

Hiya sexy, I've had a last minute change of plans and I'm now free on Sunday if you're free and you'd like to meet up? X

Jill showed us her phone and we all smiled. Game on. She replied -

Hi Ben, sorry can't do Sunday. Can do Monday, Ranji's,8? x

OK Monday at Ranji's it is. I'm really looking forward to
seeing your beautiful face in real life. I've got a great feeling about us babe. We're going to be good together xx

Jill pretended to stick her fingers down her throat and gag "Jesus wept, I can't believe anyone actually falls for this bollocks." She said. She looked at me "Whoops! Sorry Scarlett."

"It's fine, I can't believe I fell for it either." I said waving away her apology.

My phone buzzed, notification from the dating site. Message from Ben to Julie. No messing around with him that night -

Hi beautiful, I was wondering if you are free to meet up on Sunday instead of Monday? I've had a change of plans and am free now xx

"Nice to know where I come in the pecking

order!" grumbled Julie. We messaged back -

Yes, I'm free on Sunday. How's 7 at Ranji's? x

Do you fancy Italian instead? I know a lovely restaurant x

Not really, I love curry and Ranji's is supposed to be really good. Haven't had a chance to eat there yet. Can we please go there? x

OK, no problem. Ranji's it is. Looking forward to seeing your beautiful face in real life xx

"This guy is in serious need of some new lines." commented Jill.

So here's the thing, Jill's mum and dad are filthy rich and they own shares in Ranji's restaurant. Ranjit, who runs the restaurant is an old family friend and was more than happy to go along with the plan when Jill rang him explaining the situation and what we wanted to do. Julie arrived at Ranji's just before seven o'clock on Sunday to find Ben was already waiting for her at the bar. He was in full bullshittery, smarmy, fake gentleman mode, very polite, complementary and attentive - all an act as we now knew. Julie and Ben had a nice meal which Ben insisted on paying for. Just after 8.15pm as Ben was settling the bill and Ranjit was hastily clearing the table Julie excused herself to go to the ladies. In the loo she phoned Jill who happened to be waiting in the car park. Julie is pretty but Jill is simply drop dead gorgeous and she walked into the restaurant looking absolutely stunning in a sexy low cut dress that showed her gorgeous, voluptuous figure off to perfection. She spoke briefly with Ranjit who took her over to the table where Ben was still sitting. Ben was looking at his phone and looked predictably puzzled and alarmed when he glanced up and saw Jill but he soon recovered his composure, standing up and kissing her on the cheek. She grabbed his face in both her hands and gave him a big smacker right on the lips "God I'm hungry, and bloody horny!" she said, giving him a wink "I'm so very sorry I'm a little late sweetie."

"That's OK, you're not that late." he said, probably thinking actually, you're a day early but not wanting to say anything because he was completely blown away by this gorgeous woman and he just couldn't believe his luck. But what to do about Julie? He looked over, with slight panic in the direction of the ladies room.

Jill gave him a little reprieve when she excused herself saying she really needed to go to the bathroom "Would you be a sweetheart and order me a white wine, Chardonnay. Large." she asked as she walked over to the ladies where Julie was waiting for her. "Urgh, have you got any mouthwash or disinfectant in your bag? Got a bit carried away there and kissed the slimy toad. I threw up a little in my mouth but we've got him right where we want him." She told Julie.

Julie came out of the toilet and thanked Ben for the meal. "You're very welcome." he said, standing up. He was a little distracted, his brain obviously working overtime trying to figure out what to do. "Shall I walk you to your car?"

She pretended to be disappointed "Oh, OK. Was it something I said?"

"No, not at all, erm it's just that I've just got a really early start in the morning, I have to be in Birmingham for 7am. I would really like to see you again. I think you're lovely." They got to Julie's car, "Oh, I seem to have forgotten my wallet" Ben said, patting his jacket pocket as he kissed her on the cheek. "I'll just pop back in to get it. It's OK, don't wait, you get off, I'll ring you tomorrow." and giving her a distracted wave he scurried back into the restaurant.

Inside Jill was sitting waiting for him sipping her Chardonnay. "Ah, there you are, I thought I'd scared you away!" she said as he got back to the table.

"Not at all, are you kidding me? I, erm, just had to go to my car, I'd left my wallet in there." he lied.

"Now" said Jill picking up the menu "What shall we have to eat? I'm starving, are you?"

"Truthfully I'm not really all that hungry and I'm trying to keep an eye on my weight" said Ben, well he wouldn't be hungry considering he had literally just finished a three course banquet with Julie.

"Rubbish! There's nothing on you. The food here is really good. I'll order for you" said Jill. Ranjit came over and she ordered food, lots of food.

As Ben picked at his second three course Indian banquet of the evening Jill went to work on him with some world class flirting. She force fed him some very spicy chicken Jalfrezi and insisted he try the Gulab Jamun for dessert. "I'll just have a bit of yours." he said.

"Oh no you won't, I'm not sharing!" she replied. Ranjit brought over the desserts, by which point Ben was looking decidedly green but he was a sport and ate it all, with Jill's encouragement. It was time to step up the flirting even more "That was delicious" said Jill leaning over and whispering in Ben's ear, "I'm not hungry for food any more but I am hungry for this big boy" putting her hand on his crotch and squeezing his cock through his trousers. He went hard immediately.

"Shall we go to a hotel?" he suggested hopefully.

"Yes. Lets." said Jill, giving his erection another little squeeze.

Ben gulped "OK, I'll just get the bill." As Ben paid for his second Indian banquet of the evening, (it had been an expensive night so far for the poor guy) Jill fired off a quick text message to me -

```
We're on!!!!
```

"Just seeing if my friend is up for joining us, if that's OK?" Jill told Ben, explaining the text.

"Yes, yes of course." Said Ben with an enormous grin. He must have thought all his Christmases had come at once. I'll bet he was just dying to tell all his NW Big Boy pals all about this particular conquest.

They left the restaurant, Jill winking at Ranjit as they left and saying to Ben "I hope you left a tip after that delicious meal".

Time for phase three.

CHAPTER TWENTY FIVE

Julie drove straight round to my house after her 'date' with Ben. Whilst we were waiting, knowing he was preoccupied with Jill we used Ben's credentials to login to QwiKChat and went into the NW Big Boys group to investigate it further. It was truly shocking. Reading though the texts that Ben had posted about our sex life I felt humiliated and totally stupid. It also appeared that he thought himself quite the seduction guru, giving the other men tips and advice on how to get women into bed with what he called his "lovecraft". His number one tip: act like a gentleman at all times, classy women like that kind of thing. He also advised the men in the group to pretend to fall in love, shower women with attention and be tactile but not overly so. His first date tips - "A stroke of the skin, always politely ask for permission first before touching and lots of eye contact is all you need. Listen to them, even if they're really boring give them all your attention. It will inevitably lead to sex, if not on the first date then I can almost guarantee it will on the second. Of course it also helps if you've got a big dick!" I recalled our first date, remembering how he'd politely asked if he could touch my skin to see if it was as soft as it looked. How he had acted like the perfect gentleman. How he had listened intently to everything I'd said. It had been scripted right down to the smallest detail. Then of course so was our relationship and how he had 'fallen in love' with me. I had been totally played.

There was plenty more misogynistic bullshit on the group. From sharing dating profiles of women that were referred to as guaranteed 'First Date Lays' to sharing information about women that they'd had sex with so as to help other men to seduce them. Posts such as "Linda recently lost her dad, pretend you've just lost a parent too and give her loads of sympathy. Death is a great aphrodisiac." to scoring women on tit size, sexual performance and willingness to perform various sexual acts. They bragged about getting women drunk just so they could use them for sex and the various ways they dumped them afterwards when they became "too needy" or they felt the relationship was in danger of becoming too serious. These were professional men too, the majority of them were articulate, intelligent and well spoken. Some were married. They spoke of what they did with women simply as 'The Game' and challenged each other to do various things with the unsuspecting victims.

The worst thing though were the hundreds of pictures and videos of naked and semi naked women, some performing sex acts, some obviously drunk or drugged. I was sickened when I realised most of the pictures and videos looked like they'd been covertly taken. My stomach turned as I thought of the night when Ben had persuaded me to masterbate for him via video chat and I wondered if he had somehow recorded that and posted it to the group. I felt humiliated enough knowing he had shared intimate details of our sex life with these perverts just by text and was really hoping he hadn't shared any pictures or videos. I scrolled back through a few months of posts relieved when I didn't find any. I did find a screenshot of my OKCupid dating profile. I'd been marked 7/10 and Ben had been challenged with trying to get me to join in group sex with him. He'd accepted the challenge. Explained a lot.

I found plenty of evidence of Ben's recent sexual exploits with other women, especially Lola, pictures of whom he had posted. Unlike most of the others Lola was obviously posing for the pictures but whether she knew he had posted them to the group or not was a different matter. Julie and I scrolled through the group in silence for a while, I took some notes and some screenshots for evidence and then closed it down. I'd seen enough and so had Julie.

Not long afterwards we got the text message off Jill. The nearest, half decent hotel to the restaurant was the one where I had first met Ben and I knew he would take her there. We got into the car and made our way there too. Shortly afterwards we got another text message -

Room 223

The irony, it was the same room as the one we had used for our third date, maybe he got a discounted rate on it.

Julie and I got to the hotel and sat waiting in the lobby. About five minutes went by and we got another message.

Come up

We got into the lift and went up to the second floor.

Jill and Ben had arrived at the hotel about fifteen minutes previously. Ben had been looking a little peaky but Jill kept up the flirting and suggestive behaviour and there was no way he was going to turn down such an opportunity. In the hotel room she had stripped to her underwear and he had immediately gone past the point of no return. There was nothing he wouldn't have done for her at that moment in time. "Do you like what you see Ben?" she asked as she came out of the bathroom and paraded in front of him in her matching black lace bra and knickers complete with lace top hold ups.

"Oh yes" he said, licking his lips, eyes wide trying to take all of her in at once. His stomach let out a low growl "Sorry about that, the curry mustn't be agreeing with me." he said a little embarrassed.

"Are you feeling OK? Shall we leave it for tonight?" Jill asked feigning concern.

"No, no, I'll be fine" he assured her.

"Good. Now I like my men to be submissive. Do you have a problem with that?"

"No." At that moment in time I think he would have agreed to anything in order to get his end away.

"Take off your clothes."

He did as he was told discarding his clothes quickly into a pile on the chair at the side of the bed. Jill picked up her handbag and took out a large pair of black plastic cable ties. "I'm going to ride you cowgirl style then give you the best blowjob you've ever had in your life. Then when my friend gets here you're going to get a show" she promised him "but first you're going to kneel for me and then I'm going to tie you up."

He looked a little unsure at first but then he got on his knees. She stood in front of him and rubbed the top of his head for a moment giving it a little slap to finish off for good measure "Starting to look a bit sparse up there aren't we?" she commented "Now, get on the bed" She ordered. He got onto the bed and Jill tied his wrists to the frame with the cable ties. Next she got a silk scarf from her bag, climbed onto the bed straddled Ben's legs leaning into him, her breasts pushing up against his chest and tied it around his eyes. "Makes it all the more exciting don't you think?" she whispered in his ear. He nodded eagerly.

Ben's stomach started to growl again. "Erm, Jill?" he said "Is there any possibility you can untie me for a moment? I think I may need to go to the toilet."

"No Ben, no possibility at all." She said sweetly and climbed off the bed. We knocked on the door "Oh here's my friend."

Jill opened the door for me and Julie and I almost laughed out loud when I walked into the room to see Ben tied up and naked on the bed with an impressive erection and trying his hardest not to shit himself. I just about managed to keep a straight face. Setting the camera on my phone to record video I said "Hello darling, fancy seeing you here."

"Scarlett??" said Ben totally confused. "What, how, wha...oohh.." he sounded pained, his stomach growling loudly again.

"I see you've had a bit of a busy night, meeting my lovely friends Julie and Jill."

"Your friends? I don't understand. What's going on? Please untie me." He was moving his head from side to side trying to dislodge the scarf so he could see what was happening.

"Well, here's the thing, I know all about you

Ben. I know all about the QwiKChat group North West Big Boys and the fact that you have been sharing intimate details of our love life with a bunch of perverted fucktards. I know you have been shagging Lola all along, amongst others and still participating in group sex and that you still have active profiles on all the dating sites. I can't believe the arrogance of you, what were you thinking? Did you think I would never get wise to any of it?"

He just sat there, the only sound coming from him a low growling noise from his stomach. What could he say? Could hardly worm his way out of this one could he?

"What's the matter Ben, cat got your tongue?" asked Julie.

"What I can't understand though is all the lies. Why? I was happy for it just to be a sex thing, why did you turn it into a relationship, why tell me you loved me?" I continued

He was quiet for a moment maybe trying to think of a way to try to talk his way out but then he shrugged "It's what you wanted to hear." His stomach growled again, louder this time and he groaned, beads of sweat forming on his brow.

Maybe it was what I had wanted to hear. I had been hurt so badly in the past and I just longed to be loved. The times I spent with him holding me tightly and telling me I was beautiful and how much he loved me had been some of the happiest times of my life. But it had been a load of bullshit.

"Not a nice person are you really? I'd told you how badly I'd been hurt, you had your choice of women who are quite happy to participate in the kind of casual sex you enjoy but you still had to manipulate me into falling in love with you, use and humiliate me, just to earn bragging rights in some fucked up group. Well it's your turn for a bit of humiliation now. Not that this is even a fraction of the punishment you deserve. We'd best be going, things are going to be getting a little unpleasant in here. It was nice knowing you Ben. Well actually, no it wasn't." I said. I waited for his reply but it seemed that for once he didn't have anything to say. I stopped the video camera on my phone and switched it over to photo clicking a few pictures of Ben for good measure.

"Wait! You can't leave me tied up like this." cried Ben letting out a loud squelchy fart.

"Oh, we can" chuckled Jill as she got dressed "Bye Ben, it was a pleasure. Oh by the way, those laxatives I popped into your dessert should be starting to work their magic very soon. Along with all the curry you've had tonight they should help get rid of some of that shit you're full of!"

Taking one last hard look at the pitiful excuse for a man that had somehow managed to manipulate me into falling in love with him I turned and left the room.

"Don't worry, we'll call the hotel and get someone to come and free you in, oh, maybe an hour or so. Give you some time to contemplate what an utter cockwomble you are." said Jill laughing as she closed and locked the door behind us.

Down in the hotel bar we ordered a bottle of the most expensive champagne they had. "Please charge it to my room, number 223." Jill told the barman handing over the keycard.

"No problem madam." he said taking the card and swiping it. Ben's poor credit card hadn't half taken a battering that night. Sadly we could only have one small glass each as we were driving but we thoroughly enjoyed it nonetheless.

"Here's to friends, curry, sex, drink and most of all poor Ben." laughed Jill raising her glass.

"Cheers!" replied Julie and I and we all clinked our glasses together smiling at each other.

"I love it when a plan comes together." said Julie in a very bad American accent and we all laughed.

I opened the NW Big Boys group on my phone, once more logging in as Ben. Posting one of the pictures of him tied up naked on the bed with the comment "I've been challenged not to shit myself in the next hour. Don't think I'm going to make it."

CHAPTER TWENTY SIX

It had been a few weeks since the night at the hotel with Ben. Unsurprisingly I hadn't heard anything from him and I was totally happy with that. I didn't miss him one little bit and looking back couldn't believe the hold that he'd had over me. The sex, the swingers clubs, the chat group, the other women, the lies - it all just seemed like a weird dream now. I hadn't been on any dates or rejoined any of the dating sites, I really couldn't be bothered, Ben had put me off meeting men for life. Or at least for the foreseeable future.

Life went on. I was a little lonely sometimes but I decided to try my hand at writing a novel, something I'd always wanted to do and lost myself in my work. Of course I still spent lots of time with my friends. I decided to adopt a friend for Walter and had a trip to the local animal rescue centre where a tiny black female kitten chose me to be her slave. "She's a feisty one that one. Thinks she's a lion." one of the staff commented as I picked up the kitten and held her for the first time enchanted by her tiny nose and little paws. She purred as she bit my nose and licked my cheek and I knew she was the one for me. I took her home and called her Maureen. Mo immediately assumed the role of boss cat and put grumpy Walter firmly in his place by smacking him across the nose whenever he went too close to her. He was wary at first but soon fell head over paws in love with her in spite of the nose smacks. He seemed to revert back to kittenhood, chasing her around, playing with her toys and snuggling up to her - whenever she allowed him to of course. I think I even heard him purring once or twice. Perhaps Maureen could teach me a thing or two on how to deal with the male species. Jill said I was in danger of becoming a crazy old spinster cat lady but that was fine by me.

Jill's birthday arrived and we were celebrating in the pub having a grand old time on Mad Paddy's Karaoke. I was a little drunk just for a change and enthusiastically belting out a classic Divinyls number when in walked Neil. "I don't want, anybody else, when I think about you I touch myself" I sang - only ever so slightly off key - looking at him and giving him a saucy wink. He laughed at me and raised his eyebrows, I smiled back and blew him a kiss. He went to the bar and after I finished murdering the song I sat back down with Jill, Jill's girlfriend Emma, Julie and Becky.

"I heard Neil's getting married." Becky informed us.

I felt a huge jolt of jealousy at this news. "Oh? To Cheryl?" I asked trying to act nonchalant but fooling no one.

"Yes, apparently she asked him last week."

"She asked him? And he said yes?" I asked.

"That's what I've heard on the grapevine." said Becky shrugging her shoulders.

"Shame you were so infatuated with the knob with the big knob" remarked Jill "missed out on a good one there." I looked over towards the bar where Neil was standing talking to his friend Dave. She was right, I had missed out. I'd missed him I realised looking at his tousled red hair and allowing myself to entertain a very brief fantasy in which we were both naked, he was holding me kissing my neck and I was running my fingers through that fine mane before I was jolted back to reality by Sharon on the karaoke trying to make our ears bleed with her rendition of 'Jolene'.

A few minutes later Neil wandered over to our table, kissing us all on the cheek and wishing Jill a happy birthday. He asked how we were all doing.

"We're great thanks. Scarlett finally got rid of that idiot she was so infatuated with and she's single again so that's a good thing." said Jill, I kicked her under the table.

"That is good news. He wasn't good enough for her." He said looking at me. We made eye contact, he held my gaze for a moment smiling at me then I looked away feeling a bit embarrassed.

"I believe congratulations are in order." said Becky to Neil.

"Congratulations?" He asked, looking at Becky with a puzzled expression.

"Yes. You and Cheryl, getting married." replied Becky.

He laughed "No, I can assure you that's fake news, sorry. In fact I'm not seeing her anymore. She did ask me to marry her but I just couldn't see myself spending the rest of my life with a woman who thought Japan is the capital of China and had no clue who our current Prime Minister is. When I said thank you but no thank you to her proposal she went off in a huff and I've not heard from her since."

He wasn't getting married! I felt elated at this news for a moment until I realised I had fucked things up a long time ago with Neil by choosing Ben over him and I felt sad again.

"Anyway, I'll leave you lovely ladies to it. It's been a pleasure as usual." he said. We made and held eye contact again, I felt my face flush. "Bye Red." he said, winking at me then he walked back over to the bar.

"He still likes you." remarked Julie as we all watched him walk away "You should ask him out, what have you got to lose?" I really wanted to, but I wasn't brave enough. I was too scared of rejection.

"Oh, I'm happy just to be friends." I said.

"Liar!" said Jill.

It was quite late when I got back home from the pub, around one am when the taxi dropped me off and I was a little worse for wear from the drink. Walking up my path I could hear a little cry coming from the direction of the bushes. It sounded like Maureen but I was sure I'd put the lock on the cat flap so she couldn't get out. I followed the direction of the cries softly calling out to her, and there she was, shivering and scared. I picked her up, stroking her gently and speaking to her softly to calm her. "How did you get out here little one?" I'd either forgotten to lock the cat flap or she'd somehow sneaked out of the door as I was leaving. I really needed to be more careful, she was far too small to be outside. "Come on Mo, let's get you inside." she was snuggling under my chin purring, happy to see me. Once inside I checked the cat flap, surprised to see it was locked. "Well, Houdini, you must have sneaked out when I wasn't looking, going to have to keep a closer eye on you aren't I?" I said putting her gently on the floor and giving her some food. At the smell of the food Walter came sloping in so I gave him some too and chided him for not looking after his little friend better.

I got myself a glass of water, checked the doors

were locked and yawning made my way upstairs. In my bedroom I sleepily started to get undressed when I heard the click of the door closing behind me and a soft voice say “Hello Scarlett.”

It had been a while since I had last received any bizarre gifts and several months since the unnerving visit from my stalker and I’d almost forgotten all about it. Lulled into a false sense of security I had even stopped bothering to arm my alarm system because the cats were always setting it off when they were having their mad moments running around like loons. At the sound of my name I whirled around, my throat constricted in terror, which quickly turned to confusion when I saw Gina standing there.

“Gina! What..what are you doing here?” I said stammering in surprise.

“Sit on the bed Scarlett” She ordered. My momentary relief at seeing it was Gina turning back into alarm when I noticed she was holding a large, lethal looking knife in her right hand. I did as she asked sitting on the bed, I was shaking, my teeth clattering in shock, my mind whirling in confusion.

“Thank you. Now, me and you, we are going to have a little chat.” She told me.

“I don’t understand. What are you doing here? What do you want? How did you get in?”

“You are a threat to me. Me and Ben, I can’t afford to let it go on any longer.” she told me inexplicably. I opened my mouth to speak but she shushed me. "Ben is mine. You can't have him."

She obviously hadn't got the memo that Ben and I were well and truly over. "I don't want him Gina, honestly I don't. We're over. We've been over for a while."

"Don't lie to me bitch." she said speaking in a quiet, calm, monotone voice, almost friendly as though we were just chit chatting about the weather. I think I would have preferred it if she'd have shouted at me, the fact that she seemed so chilled out unnerved me even more.

"Please, Gina, put the knife down, let's talk about this."

"I'll do the talking, you shut up and listen. It's been going on far too long, you and him. He loves you. I can't have that. I'm not losing everything I have, my beautiful home, my Ben because of you. We're getting married."

"Honestly, I'm not seeing Ben anymore. He didn't love me, it was all lies. I've not seen him in weeks."

"Why should I believe you?" she said holding the knife up to her face studying it intently. She turned it around, the light reflecting off the blade and sending a shiver of terror through me. Going off the blank expression on her face the cheese had well and truly slid off her cracker.

"It's the truth, I swear it is. Anyway he wouldn't leave you. He promised you that he will stay with you and I believe he will."

She let out a little laugh "He thinks I'm dying.

I may be sick but I'm a long way off dying. It's the only way I could stop him from ending it with me. That and letting him shag whoever he wants to. That's OK, he's never liked any of them all that much, at least until you came along. He's never brought anyone to meet me before. He must be serious about you."

"I can assure you he wasn't. I was just another notch on the bedpost. He only agreed to let me meet you because I insisted on it."

From the corner of my eye I noticed my phone lighting up, Neil was ringing me, luckily I had put it on silent as I usually did when I was getting ready for bed. I looked at Gina who was staring into the distance with that disturbing blank expression on her face. I was able to press the accept call button without her noticing. "Listen to me Gina, don't say anything, just listen to me. Please put the knife down" I said urgently in a slightly louder voice looking at Gina but hoping Neil would hear me, get the message and not think it was just some kind of joke. "It's not too late for you to leave my home. Put the knife down and just go. I promise I won't tell anyone. Let's talk about this. Put it down, I promise I won't call the police."

Gina stood still just staring into the distance for a moment longer then sighed "I don't know. I just don't know about anything anymore. If he's not been with you, then where has he been going?" She looked over at me. I stole a quick glance at my phone panicking that it would still be lit up and she would notice but thankfully the screen was dark. Please let Neil be calling the police I thought.

"He could be anywhere, he has quite the collection of girlfriends." I told her.

"I knew you were different when I saw your profile. Not just a sex thing like the rest of them. I sent the gifts thinking you would tell him about them and he would get jealous and end it with you. The he brought you to meet me and I knew for sure it wasn't just a sex thing."

"But it was just a sex thing to him. I was just a bit more of a challenge. That group he was in - North West Big Boys, they'd given him the challenge to find someone like me and try to turn me into a swinger." I explained "He never loved me, it was all lies, it was all just a game to him. He didn't care if someone else was sending me gifts or even if I was sleeping with someone else. In fact he wanted me to, he just wanted to know the details like some kind of sexual vampire."

She seemed to consider this for a moment. "When did you last see him?" she asked

"It's about four or five weeks ago."

"And it's over?"

"It's most definitely over, I promise you. I want nothing more to do with him after I found out what he is truly like."

A few more seconds passed that seemed like a lifetime and then a light seemed to come on in her mind. She looked at the knife as if she was seeing it for the first time "Oh!" She said as if she was surprised to see it and dropped it on the floor. "Right then. That's OK. Sorry. Bye." she said and left.

I waited a few moments, then tried to stand up but I couldn't, my legs were shaking too much. I couldn't even pick up my phone because my hands were shaking too much too. I heard a noise from downstairs and my heart leaped into my mouth in terror again thinking she had come back to finish the job but then I heard Neil shout "Scarlett? Where are you?"

I tried to shout back to tell him I was in the bedroom but I couldn't find my voice and burst into tears instead. He came bursting into the bedroom and had a quick look to check that there was no one there other than me. "Has she gone?" he asked. I nodded. He knelt beside the bed, wrapped me in his arms and held me until the shakes and the tears subsided and the police turned up. There were a few awkward moments when the police burst in grabbing Neil and pushing him against the wall with his hands behind his back but I managed to explain that he was in fact my saviour and tell them who the intruder had been. They apologised and let him go immediately but he was a great sport about it telling them they had no need to apologise because they were only doing their jobs. They searched my house to make sure Gina had definitely gone, she had. I gave them her's and Ben's address and they found her there half an hour later. They told me she had been totally flummoxed by them turning up and was unaware that she had done anything wrong. They arrested her and she was sent to a secure unit for psychiatric evaluation. There was no sign of a break in but the kitchen door had been open when Neil arrived. I knew I had locked it and was stumped at first as to how she had gotten in but then I noticed that my spare kitchen door key was missing from the hook where it usually lived. The only thing I could think of was that she had sneaked in and taken it when I was in the back garden one day maybe. I had changed my front door lock but stupidly changing the kitchen door lock hadn't even entered my mind.

It was creeping up to 4am once the police had taken my statement, bagged up the knife for evidence and left. Neil stayed with me the whole time, feeding me strong sweet tea and holding my hand. Just being there. I thanked him for saving my life.

"Well I hardly saved your life, she'd gone by the time I got here." he pointed out.

"Yes but she could have still been here, she might have been, you turning up may well have scared her off." I said "I'm just so happy that you rang when you did and that you copped on to what was going on and came over. Anyway, why were you ringing me?"

"Well, I was wondering if you would consider

dating a mere mortal now you are no longer with your sex God?" He replied. I laughed, a little too hard then, to my embarrassment, I started to cry again and boy am I an ugly crier.

"Well that wasn't quite the reaction I was hoping for!" Neil said "Are you alright?"

"I'm OK" I said but I wasn't. Not really. The shock kicked in again and I started to shiver uncontrollably.

He pulled me into his arms again and held me close for a long time, kissing the top of my head and telling me it was going to be OK. I realised, this right here was all I'd ever wanted. Outwardly I was a confident woman enjoying life but inside I was a lonely, scared little girl who just needed to feel loved, to feel safe in someone's arms and for someone to tell me everything was going to be alright when the world was just too much to handle.

"Will you stay with me tonight? Please? Just as a friend if you like?" I asked into his now soggy chest once I'd gotten the sobbing under control.

"Don't you worry Red, I'm going nowhere." he replied. He put his hand under my chin, gently raising my face towards his and gave me a long, passionate kiss that was decidedly not platonic and made me shiver all over again but for a different reason. "I must say though" he said studying my face when we came up for air "you're not a pretty sight when you've been crying!" I laughed and elbowed him in the ribs.

Neil stayed that night. He didn't tell me he loved me. He didn't tell me I was beautiful. He didn't call me 'babe' but he held me and made me safe and wanted. We didn't make love when we first crawled into bed, we were far too tired after the police left but we made up for it later that morning. Again that afternoon, and again later that evening just for good measure. Was he good? Let's just say he is more than adequate in the trouser department and an excellent lover I have no complaints. Did he give me the happy ending I'd been craving? He certainly did that day, more than once. So what happened next? Well, let's just say there's truth in Shakesphere's saying 'The course of true love never runs smoothly' and there were quite a few surprises in store for me.

But that, my friends, is another story!

(not quite) The End

AFTERWORD

The characters and incidents portrayed in this story are fictitious. The group "NW Big Boys" isn't real however there are groups like this, and worse, that do exist in real life. No matter your age if you are dating strangers you are vulnerable and should always take great care. This goes for men as well as women. You should never agree to do anything you feel uncomfortable with or feel coerced into doing something against your will. Dating sites are a great way of meeting people and there are many, many genuine people on dating sites who are there for genuine reasons, but please be aware there are some that aren't. You should always trust your instincts. There are many scams operating, some obvious, some not quite so. Enjoy dating but always be aware unscrupulous people do exist who will exploit you if given the opportunity. To all of those who are looking for love, stay safe and I hope you find what it is you are looking for x

COFESSIONS OF A SERIAL DATER

Follow Scarlett on her journey looking for love and more importantly great sex, something that has missing from her life for far too long.

Delete, Block, Next...

Meet Scarlett. Newly single, disillusioned with love, skint, wrong side of 40, a bit fat but amazing tits. She's negotiating the pitfalls of modern dating looking for a satisfying tumble between the sheets a couple of times a week with someone who's face doesn't want to make her vomit. There appears to be plenty on offer but after weeding out the not rights, the scammers, the clinically insane and those with significant others just looking for a bit on the side the pickings are actually actually a little meagre. Will she find what she is looking for or she condemned to a life of shit sex the only orgasms coming courtesy of her friends with batteries?

Ever dated? Ever had sex? Ever been stupidly

drunk? Then this is the story for you!

Playing By The Rules

After a year of dating mishaps and romantic disasters Scarlett finally meets Ben. He's not much to look at but he's certainly providing her with the exceptional sex life she's been craving. Hurrah! The only problem is he keeps trying to push her further out of her comfort zone, she's convinced he's lying to her about her personal life and she thinks she may be falling in love with him which is against the rules. How far will she go to keep hold of him? Will she find out the truth that he's been hiding from her? And who the hell keeps sending her weird gifts that are getting stranger and stranger...

Printed in Great Britain
by Amazon

40665207R00135